No way out . . .

"I don't want to hear another word about Tom Watts," the masked man shouted. "He's completely ruined everything. He was supposed to ride back in the van and die with the rest of your no-good friends."

"*Die?* What are you talking about?" Elizabeth stuttered. "What's the matter with you? Are you insane?" Her heart started to pound, and a shiver ran up and down her spine.

"Don't you *ever* call me insane!" the man screamed. Then he laughed. "But maybe it's better that Watts live and know that when it comes to love, he's a born loser."

Elizabeth felt her body turning icy cold. There was something about the man's tone. She'd heard that voice before.

But only in her worst nightmares had she expected to hear it again.

Bantam Books in the Sweet Valley University series
Ask your bookseller for the books you have missed

And don't miss these
Sweet Valley University Thriller Editions:

SWEET VALLEY UNIVERSITY™

THRILLER EDITION

He's Watching You

Written by
Laurie John

Created by
FRANCINE PASCAL

BANTAM BOOKS
NEW YORK · TORONTO · LONDON · SYDNEY · AUCKLAND

RL 6, age 12 and up

HE'S WATCHING YOU
A Bantam Book / May 1995

Sweet Valley High® *and Sweet Valley University*™
are trademarks of Francine Pascal
Conceived by Francine Pascal
Produced by Daniel Weiss Associates, Inc.
33 West 17th Street
New York, NY 10011

ISBN: 0-553-56689-X

Published simultaneously in the United States and Canada

Bantam Books are published by Bantam Books, a division of Bantam
Doubleday Dell Publishing Group, Inc. Its trademark, consisting of the
words "Bantam Books" and the portrayal of a rooster, is Registered in
U.S. Patent and Trademark Office and in other countries. Marca
Registrada. Bantam Books, 1540 Broadway, New York, New York 10036.

PRINTED IN THE UNITED STATES OF AMERICA

OPM   0 9 8 7 6 5 4 3 2 1

To Judy and Alan Adler

Chapter One

"It'll be good for you to get out," Elizabeth Wakefield said in a bright voice.

Her twin sister, Jessica, held up a yellow cotton ribbed sweater and frowned at her reflection in the mirror. "I guess," she mumbled. She threw the sweater impatiently on her bed and pulled a red knit sheath from the closet. "I just look terrible in everything," she complained. "It makes it hard to get excited about going anywhere."

Elizabeth sat down on her bed. "You don't look terrible, but you do look unhappy. Are you OK?"

Jessica sighed and sat down on her own bed. "I don't really know."

"It's going to take some time to get over all this," Elizabeth said quietly. She moved over to

1

Jessica's bed and sat down beside her, giving her a quick hug. There was a strained, white area around Jessica's mouth that made Elizabeth's heart ache.

Jessica had shown incredible courage when she took the stand against James Montgomery, the football player who had sexually assaulted her during a date. But now that it was all over, she looked fragile and exhausted.

Elizabeth brushed Jessica's long blond hair off her shoulder and went over to her bulging closet. She scanned the contents and then pulled out a pair of white wool trousers and a black-and-white tank top with a matching sweater. "Here. This outfit looks great on you." She winked at her sister. "Now, come on. Try to look happy. Tom's taking us out to brunch to cheer you up, and you'll hurt his feelings if you don't look like you're having fun. You know how sensitive he is."

Jessica smiled. "You're so lucky to have Tom," she commented.

"*We're* lucky to have Tom," Elizabeth answered.

Jessica lifted her eyebrows as if she wasn't completely sure that was true. "I don't know. He sure teases me a lot."

"He's taking us to The Green Duck for brunch," Elizabeth said.

Jessica's eyes opened a little wider, and she

let out a low whistle. "You're right. We *are* lucky to have Tom," she agreed with a laugh. She stuffed the pants and sweater back into the closet. "This isn't nice enough for The Green Duck." She frowned slightly at Elizabeth's khaki pants and pink cardigan sweater. "And neither is that. Here's the deal. I'll try to cheer up if you'll change into the gold silk pants and jacket Mom and Dad gave you for Christmas."

"It's a deal," Elizabeth answered, unbuttoning the cardigan.

Within minutes, Jessica was busy at the mirror, humming as she applied her makeup.

Elizabeth watched her twin with a mixture of concern and amusement. Jessica was still emotionally bruised after her ordeal, and she had her good days and her bad days. But the prospect of an elegant brunch at Sweet Valley's finest French restaurant seemed to be having the desired effect—Jessica's mood was better than it had been in weeks. Elizabeth sent up a little silent prayer of thanks for Tom. He'd known that Elizabeth was worried about her sister, and the outing had been his idea.

You look like you could use a little TLC, too, he had added. *Everything OK?*

Elizabeth had insisted she was fine, unwilling to talk about the horrible nightmare that she

3

seemed unable to shake. One night Elizabeth had woken up in a cold sweat, terrified for her life. She'd dreamt that William White, the classmate who had headed a pseudo-fascist rightwing organization on campus—and tried to murder her—was at large at Sweet Valley University again. In the dream, William was watching her every move, waiting for the perfect opportunity to kill her.

Elizabeth shook her head vigorously, reminding herself that she was safe now. After the murder attempt, William had been confined to an institution for the criminally insane. Unfortunately, just knowing that William was still alive was enough to keep Elizabeth constantly on edge. And recently, her fear was permeating her life—and her dreams. The memory of William's handsome but obsessed face caused her to shiver.

"Something wrong, Liz?" Jessica asked.

Elizabeth shook her head. "Just chilly," she said firmly. Jessica already had enough to worry about. And Elizabeth knew that if she talked to Jessica about her nightmare, she'd wind up talking about the notes.

Her stomach churned. Some prankster with a sick sense of humor had really been trying to push her buttons lately—and succeeding. She'd been receiving strange notes with quotes from Shakespeare sonnets on them. The last one had been especially chilling:

Make but my name thy love, and love that still,
And then thou lov'st me, for my name is Will.

Elizabeth closed her eyes and remembered the Barbie doll that had been left for her to find in the library. A doll hanging from a noose. Elizabeth pressed her lips grimly together. She had her theories about who was behind the stunts, but she was unwilling to take any action at this point. Even though she was angry about being the target of such cruel jokes, she felt more pity than anger at the prankster. The person was obviously very troubled.

Elizabeth pulled on her gold silk pants, then shrugged on the slim-fitting matching jacket. She picked up her brush and pulled it through her long, thick blond hair. For once, she looked almost as polished and elegant as Jessica.

Although the twins were identical on the outside—from their silky blond hair and blue-green eyes to the matching dimples in their left cheeks—no two girls were less alike.

Elizabeth favored jeans, T-shirts, baseball caps, serious fiction, and challenging classes.

Jessica, on the other hand, was devoting her freshman year at Sweet Valley University to the things *she* considered important—fashion, fun, and men.

Unfortunately, most of her experiences with men had not turned out as well as Elizabeth's relationship with Tom Watts, a handsome sophomore and fellow reporter and broadcast journalist at the campus news station.

There was a knock at the door, and Elizabeth hurried to open it. She took a long look at Tom and began to laugh. "Where did you get that tie?"

Tom gave Elizabeth a soft kiss on the cheek. "Is there something wrong with my tie?" he asked dryly.

Jessica hurried over to Elizabeth's side and began to giggle. In the middle of Tom's tie was a neon-colored caricature of a football player.

"What do you think, Jess?" Elizabeth joked. "Will they let him into The Green Duck in that tie?"

"Yeah. But they might make him pay in advance."

Tom laughed and straightened the knot at his throat. "This tie was a gift," he announced in a voice of injured dignity.

"I know it's the thought that counts," Elizabeth said with a laugh, "but what were they thinking?"

Tom smiled. "I happen to like this tie." He smoothed it fondly. "A couple of the guys gave it to me last year after one of the games. Believe it or not, it's my only tie."

Tom Watts had been an NCAA superstar, a college football player with a guaranteed professional career ahead of him. But when his family had been killed on the way to a game, he had dropped out of athletics and turned his attention to academics and his work at the WSVU television station.

Tom seemed confident and emotionally secure, but Elizabeth knew that he had never really recovered from the loss. The way Tom saw it, he had been a self-absorbed egomaniac—getting all his highs from seeing his family in the stands and putting too much pressure on them to attend the games. According to Tom, if his parents hadn't felt as though they *had* to make the trip to watch him play, they would still be alive.

Elizabeth had pointed out to him time after time that watching him play had probably been as much of a thrill for them as playing had been for him. There was no way he could have stopped them from coming to the games.

But Tom refused to absolve himself. And

Elizabeth knew there was nothing she could do for Tom until he was willing to accept that he wasn't responsible for the tragic car accident.

Still, the football tie was a good sign. Although Tom continued to enjoy sports and followed them as a spectator, sometimes the subject of his former role as a football star could make him distant and unapproachable.

Today, Tom looked far from distant. He stood in the room, teasing Jessica about her puffy, sprayed-up hairdo, and Jessica giggled, ribbing him back about his horrible tie.

"Come on," Tom said, glancing at his watch. "We've got reservations, and I'm hungry." He gave them both an inquiring look. "Hamburgers all around?"

"No way!" Elizabeth shouted.

"You're not getting off that easy," Jessica countered. "I'm ordering shrimp."

"I'm having something very French with lots of cream and butter," Elizabeth said, pushing her worries and fears to the back of her mind. She was determined to put on a happy face for their brunch. If Tom and Jessica could make the effort, so could she.

Tom opened the door and followed the girls into the hallway. "Darn! I *knew* I should have suggested pizza."

*　　　*　　　*

William White gazed moodily at the acousti-
cal tiles that lined the ceiling of his cell. His
mind flickered from one subject to another, but
he seemed unable to focus.

William sat up on his bed and cracked his
knuckles impatiently. He was bored. Bored with
the routine of the quiet and expensive asylum.
Bored with his ridiculous "therapy" and the
idiot doctors who had the idea he needed to be
cured of something. He needed to get out of
this purgatory and experience the exhilaration of
freedom.

William crossed the room and grasped the
bars on the little grate in the door of his cell. He
fought the impulse to shake them like a gorilla.
God! If you weren't insane when you arrived in
this place, you would be by the time you'd been
there a week or two.

Looking at inkblots. Answering a lot of im-
pertinent questions about one's childhood.
They tried to make him feel like a freak and a
criminal simply because he was one of those rare
individuals who chose to bypass the conven-
tional moralities that bound ordinary people
and pursue life on his own terms. A life that
would be empty beyond endurance without
Elizabeth.

"Elizabeth!" he said softly, enjoying the sound of her name. If only he could talk to her.

William stood on tiptoe and peered impatiently into the empty hallway. He turned angrily and began to pace. This situation was becoming intolerable. It was time to act. Even though he was able to leave the institution almost daily, every time he tried to get close to Elizabeth, someone interfered. Some friend. Or some . . . William ground his teeth in fury as he thought about Tom Watts. That lout. That lowlife. That scum.

Tom Watts had to die. That was all there was to it. No other punishment was suitable. For that matter, anyone who had ever come between William and Elizabeth had to die.

He sat down on his bed, his mind happily occupied now as he mentally reviewed the list of people that surrounded Elizabeth and effectively formed a barrier to their mutual love: There was Jessica, of course. She would have to go. And that Enid, or Alexandra, or whatever she was calling herself these days. Winston Egbert and Denise Waters. Maia Stillwater.

Then there was that Danny Wyatt. Danny had been at the root of so many of William's problems, it would be a pleasure to finally get rid of him.

For a long time, William had tried to unite the members of his secret society against a common enemy. He had hoped that Danny Wyatt would prove to be a serviceable common enemy. But Danny was a handsome African-American and an excellent student. He had commanded Elizabeth's respect and earned her sympathy. And that had been the beginning of William's downfall.

His beloved had made it her business to expose the inner workings of William's secret society. It had brought them into conflict and driven a wedge between them.

Danny would pay for that, William vowed. He would pay dearly.

Isabella Ricci, too. From what William had observed, Danny and Isabella had become a very close couple in recent weeks. She would have to die with him.

William lay back down on his bunk, completely engrossed in his planning and scheming. His mind moved faster and faster as he formulated a foolproof, murderous plan for . . .

He jumped to his feet when he heard the faint metallic click of the lock on his door. "Andrea!" he cried as the door swung open.

Andrea's dark, plain, and rather sullen face broke into a smile. "Sorry I'm late," she said, a faint bit of color creeping into her cheeks and animating her unpleasantly bovine expression. "I had a dental appointment." She pulled a piece of paper from her pocket. "Here's the week's schedule of bed checks and therapy sessions."

William snatched the paper from her hand and studied it through narrowed eyes. Andrea routinely provided him with this information, which enabled him to sneak in and out of the asylum with relative ease.

"You're not angry with me for being late, are you?" she asked.

William forced his lips to curve into a caressing smile. "I was worried," William said in a serious voice. "I thought perhaps you had abandoned me."

"Oh, no," she answered gravely. "Never! I could never . . ." She broke off as if she was too moved to speak.

He gripped her upper arm and gave it an intimate squeeze. "I need your help again—and the keys to your car."

"You're going out?" she said, pouting. "Today?"

William lifted one haughty eyebrow. He hated her incessant questioning.

"I don't want you to go out today," she protested. "It's my birthday. I thought maybe we could take a walk on the grounds after your therapy."

Ahhhh. So it was her birthday. Oh, well. Women were sentimental about birthdays. It was probably best to humor her. He put his arms around her and held her tightly against his chest. "It's for your country," he said in a deep voice. "Believe me, darling, I would never leave you today if there were any other way"—he pushed her back and stared straight into her eyes—"but the forces of evil never sleep."

"Terrorists again?" she asked.

William nodded solemnly. Andrea was like all plain and lonely girls—gullible. It had been no trick at all to convince her that he was a political prisoner incarcerated to prevent the exposure of terrorist agents in highly placed government positions.

Her face softened, and he could hear the jingle of her keys as she toyed with them in her pocket. William's fingers itched to grab her shoulders and shake her. The sooner he was out of this trap and no longer dependent on Andrea, the better. But for now, he needed her trust.

"Andrea," he said in a coaxing tone, "we can't put ourselves first." He put his hand under her chin and tipped her face upward. "No matter how much we want to be together, protecting freedom and democracy has to be our first priority."

She relented. Her face relaxed, and she fluttered her sparse eyelashes. "Oh, William. You're so brave. Aren't you ever afraid? Of anything?"

"Never," he replied truthfully.

He felt her small hand tuck a set of keys into his. "Put these in your pocket," she said, opening the door to his cell and standing aside so he could pass. "After your therapy, I'll meet you in the craft room and walk you past the attendants."

"Thank you," he whispered. "You're a wonderful woman." He brushed an imaginary tear from his cheek. "And a great American," he added in a whisper.

"Todd!"

Todd turned and smiled. A guy walked toward him with his hand extended. "How are you?" Todd said in a pleasant voice, reaching out to shake hands.

"Great," the guy answered. "Just great!" He smiled broadly and adjusted his baseball hat, from which a brown ponytail dangled. "You probably don't remember me. My name's Henry. I went to Big Mesa High, and I was a

14

couple of years ahead of you. But I sure remember seeing you play. Wow! I'm, like, such a basketball fan and you were so awesome in high school. So whatcha doin' these days? Slam-dunkin' for SVU?"

Todd smiled ruefully. How did you tell a complete stranger you'd been bounced from the game for supposedly accepting illegal payments? He didn't like to advertise the fact that he'd turned into a grade-A loser. "Not really," he said in a careful voice. "A couple of things came up, and I'm taking a season off."

Henry was immediately contrite and concerned. "No way, man. That's terrible. You're a total star."

Todd darted a look at his reflection in the window of the card shop. He didn't look like a star—he looked terrible. He hadn't bothered to shave for a few days, and his eyes were slightly bloodshot. He had a Western Civ lecture in an hour. If he hurried back to campus now, he'd have time to clean up a little. . . .

"If you've got time for some coffee, I sure would like to hear about some of the games you played."

"Gee," Todd began, "I'd really like to but . . ."

"Oh, come on, dude," Henry pleaded. "The coffee's on me. And I'm such a total fan. I saw

15

you play early in the season against State. Wow! You barreled down that court in the last four seconds and"—the guy snapped his fingers—"it was nothin' but net. What's that feel like?"

Todd remembered the play. When the ball had fallen through the net, the crowd's cheers had echoed through the gym. He'd been on top of the world.

Todd studied the guy's hopeful face. It was nice to be a hero again—to somebody. "I guess I could use a cup of coffee," Todd said.

"Great. How 'bout this place?"

Todd followed his fan into the doorway of a small coffee shop, and then over to a table in the back. When the waitress came over, Todd waved away the menus she was holding. "Two coffees, please."

The waitress nodded. By the time she returned with the coffee, Henry had prompted Todd to recount his favorite basketball story. The guy was all right, Todd decided, as he eased into one of his favorite anecdotes.

As Henry listened, Todd told one story after another. When he happened to catch sight of the clock on the wall, he couldn't believe how much time had passed. "Oh, no!" he cried, practically jumping out of his seat.

"What's the matter?"

16

"I've got to go. Listen, thanks for the coffee, but I've got a class in ten minutes. I'm going to be late."

"No sweat, man. It's a five-minute drive."

"Yeah, but I'm walking."

"Take my car," Henry said casually. He reached into the pocket of his jacket and pulled out a set of keys.

"Oh, I couldn't do that," Todd answered quickly, putting his napkin down. "But you could drive me."

Henry shook his head. "I can't. I've got to meet a guy here in a couple of minutes. Take the car, and then just bring it back here when your class is over. I'll wait."

Todd hesitated. Western Civ was an important class. He'd been slipping in the academic department lately—largely because of too many late, beer-filled nights.

"Go on, guy. Take the car."

Todd grinned. Not only was it nice to be admired again, it was nice to be trusted. He hadn't inspired too much confidence in his friends lately. "Thanks," Todd said, reaching out to take the keys. He looked out the window at the cars parked along the curb. "Which one is it?"

"Right out there," Henry answered, pointing toward the street. "The green Mazda."

"Hello?" Noah lifted his hand and waved it past Alexandra's eyes. "Are you in there?"

Alexandra fluttered her eyelashes and focused on Noah's handsome face. They were sitting at Sweet Valley Sidewalk Café, sipping cappuccino and enjoying the sunny sky and light mountain breeze. "Sorry. I just got distracted." She lifted her coffee cup and nodded toward the other side of the street.

Noah turned in his little café chair just in time to see Tom, Elizabeth, and Jessica disappear inside the front door of The Green Duck. "Wow!" he said. "The Green Duck is pretty big stuff. Is it somebody's birthday?"

Alexandra shook her head. "Nope."

"Are you sure?"

"Elizabeth and I were best friends all through high school," Alexandra said with a laugh. "I know when her birthday is."

"Well, maybe it's Tom's birthday," Noah suggested. "The Green Duck is definitely a celebration-type place." His eyes crinkled in a smile, and Alexandra smiled back.

She felt as though every day was a day for celebrating when she was with Noah. Until they'd started dating, her freshman year had been an emotional roller coaster. Now she felt

18

that she was finally mending and becoming a real person.

Alexandra had decided that going to college was her opportunity to create a new identity for herself. First, she'd gone from being plain old Enid Rollins, best friend of Elizabeth Wakefield, to being Alexandra Rollins, Ms. Campus Popularity and girlfriend of Mark Gathers, SVU's biggest basketball star.

But Mark had decided to leave school after a sports-recruiting scandal, leaving Alexandra feeling deflated and abandoned. She'd tried to lift her spirits by drinking and clinging to Todd Wilkins, Elizabeth's ex-boyfriend.

"So how are you and Elizabeth getting along?" Noah asked.

Alexandra bit her lip. Noah knew a lot about her—and a lot about how difficult her friendship with Elizabeth had been since they arrived at college. "We've been talking a lot more lately. I think she's ready to forgive me for being such a bad friend."

Alexandra closed her eyes. She felt awful about the way she had behaved. She'd been so caught up in changing her image when they'd arrived at SVU that she'd completely shut Elizabeth out of her life. Alex doubted that Elizabeth would ever totally trust her again. She wished there were some way to repair the damage to their friendship.

Noah took a sip of his coffee. "It's hard when old friends change," he commented. "It's hard to accept the new them, and hard to get them to accept the new you."

"It's also hard not to feel responsible when an old friend isn't doing so hot," she added softly.

"Look, Alexandra," Noah said, leaning across the table and taking her hand. "If you're talking about Todd, he's practically a grown man. He didn't treat you much like a friend. And he's not treating himself very well these days either."

Alexandra shrugged. "I just hate watching somebody who had so much go down the drain."

"There's not much you can do for him until he's ready to put down the bottle."

Suddenly, a squeal of tires, followed by a scream, interrupted their conversation. Noah jumped from his chair and dove protectively toward Alexandra, pulling her from her chair and pushing her behind him.

In front of their horrified eyes, a green Mazda veered toward the curb and plowed into several parked cars.

Noah released Alexandra abruptly and raced

toward the Mazda. Moments later, she gasped as Noah and a couple of women helped the driver out the driver's side. "Todd!" she cried, running toward the street.

The wail of police sirens filled the air. Before Alexandra reached the curb, four uniformed policemen had jumped from their squad cars and were converging on Todd.

"Sir, may I see your license, please?" the tallest one asked. As Alexandra watched, another studied the plates on the Mazda and returned to his car, lifting the radio to his lips.

Todd held out his license with a shaking hand. "I don't know what happened," he said in a weak voice. "The steering wheel just . . ."

"Sir, have you had anything to drink?" the policeman asked, interrupting him.

Todd's face immediately darkened. "No," he answered curtly.

Alexandra saw the policeman studying Todd. He looked terrible—like someone who'd been drinking.

The crowd was growing larger, and there were a lot of muttered conversations among the bystanders.

"Would you mind stepping over to the car?" the policeman said.

"What for?" Todd demanded.

"I'd like you to take a Breathalyzer test."

"I am *not* drunk."

"The Breathalyzer will confirm that, sir." The policeman put his hand on Todd's arm, and Todd yanked it violently away. "I *said* I'm not drunk!"

Noah stepped forward. "Todd, I think you should cooper—"

A policeman put a restraining hand against Noah's chest. "Let us handle this, please."

Todd clenched his fists. "There was something wrong with the wheel," he insisted. "I didn't do anything wrong. I haven't been drinking. I . . ."

The policeman at the radio sprang from the squad car and hurried toward the group with his hand on his gun. "It's a seven-oh-four," he shouted.

Immediately, two of the policemen moved toward Todd. One of them grabbed his arm, twisted it around, and slammed him against the Mazda.

"What are you doing?" Todd yelled. He struggled against the car, but one of the policemen shoved him back into place. "This car was reported stolen two hours ago," the policeman answered. "You're under arrest."

"I didn't steal this car!" Todd shouted. He

pushed against the policemen who'd begun to guide him toward the police car. "I didn't steal anything. Let go of me!"

Tears were streaming down Alexandra's face now. It was hard to watch the hero of her high school days being stuffed into the backseat of a police car.

She wiped her tears away as Noah came trotting toward her. "It looks like he's in trouble. But it could have been worse. At least nobody was hurt."

As the huge crowd gradually drifted away, Alexandra saw Elizabeth's unhappy face watching the police car drive off down the street.

Elizabeth caught Alexandra's eye and walked over to join her and Noah. "I saw it through the window and came out when I saw the police. What happened?"

Noah nodded with his head toward the wrecked cars along the curb. "Todd came screeching around that corner, hit those cars, and was apparently driving a stolen car."

Elizabeth pressed her lips together. "Was he drunk?" she asked.

"I don't know," Alexandra answered after an uncomfortable pause. "He said he wasn't."

Elizabeth sighed heavily. "Well, so much for brunch. She shoved her purse up under her arm.

I'm going downtown to see about Todd."

"I'll come with you," Alexandra offered.

"Would you excuse us a second?" Noah asked Elizabeth. Then he took Alexandra's fingers and pulled her gently to the side. "What are you doing?" he asked quietly.

"I'm going to the police station with Elizabeth," she answered.

Noah frowned. "He's not your problem," he said in a neutral tone.

"No. But he's my friend. And so is Elizabeth. Or at least they used to be my friends." She pecked him on the cheek. "Don't worry. I'll call you when I get back to campus."

Noah watched Alexandra's car pull out of the parking lot at the end of the street and lifted his hand in a wave. He couldn't help feeling a little uncomfortable about Alexandra's rushing down to the police station to help Todd. Was it really her job to stand by Elizabeth's side while she bailed her old boyfriend out of jail?

Noah stood at the perimeter of the small group that was still assessing the damage to the cars. He crossed his arms and leaned against the wall of the café. When Alexandra talked about her high school days, Todd's name came up a lot. Todd was down and out right now, but he was still a good-looking guy.

On the other hand, Noah knew he was a pretty good-looking guy, too. Still, some women liked the kind of drama that went along with trouble and the men who caused it.

If Alexandra was one of those women, he didn't stand a chance. He wasn't a drinker, and he definitely wasn't into driving stolen cars and getting into loud arguments with cops. In fact, he'd never had any dealings with the police at all.

"Sir. You were here when the accident occurred. May I get your name and ask you a few questions?"

Noah turned and saw a very serious, very stern police officer standing at his elbow holding a notepad.

Never had any dealings with the police—*until now,* he mentally amended.

Right now, Alexandra was attracted to him because he was easy to be with and nonjudgmental. But he couldn't help wondering how long a tame guy like him could hold her attention.

William lowered the newspaper that he had used to shield himself from view and watched the milling, gossiping crowd across the street. If only he could have been here to see it. He had run all the way from the coffee shop two blocks away, but he had just missed the crash.

He'd heard it, though. He'd savored the

sound of metal against metal as Todd sideswiped one car after another.

Luckily, he'd arrived in time to watch Todd struggling and arguing with two large, and rather gruff, policemen.

William smiled. Todd had been ridiculously easy to manipulate. So easy William almost felt ashamed of himself. He chuckled aloud. A little flattery, and Todd had fallen right into William's hands. Good grief! He had been easier to manipulate than a woman.

William folded up the newspaper and stuffed it into the back pocket of his jeans. He was through for the day. But he wasn't through with Todd Wilkins yet.

He wasn't through with Andrea, either. He turned the corner and headed toward a gift shop. He'd surprise her with a card. Something with a terrible poem full of vulgar, cheap sentiment would be best. And if he handled things correctly, she wouldn't be upset about her wrecked car—which he had reported stolen two hours ago.

A sugary card. A few kisses. It wouldn't be too hard to convince her that a car was a small sacrifice to make for her country.

Besides, she was insured.

*   *   *

Celine Boudreaux thoughtfully tapped the long red nail of her index finger against the rim of her coffee cup. She loved sitting in the window booths of the Lamplight coffee shop. She could watch the world go by from this window. It was almost better than a soap opera.

She had seen Alexandra Rollins and Noah Pearson stroll past, holding hands and looking very much like an item. Then they'd taken their seats at the café across the street and talked intently across the table. The whole time, Alexandra had leaned closer and closer—as if she just couldn't get enough of listening to him. That was just about the oldest trick in the book. But it worked. Men just ate it up, and Noah was no exception.

Celine took another long drag on her cigarette as a couple of girls from her English class waved from the other side of the window. Celine languidly lifted her fingers and gave them a brief and uninterested flutter. It was hard for her to get excited over being greeted by a bunch of girls. Celine had never gotten along well with other girls—especially her ex-roommate, Elizabeth Wakefield. Princess Prude had made Celine's life miserable.

Celine lifted a thumb and carefully wiped a smudge of thick black eyeliner away. Girls like

Elizabeth gave her a major pain. Sweet. Honest. Studious. Bleh!

So far, it had been a pleasure helping William White terrorize her.

Celine moodily stubbed out her cigarette and then lit another. In spite of the silly ponytail and the sunglasses, she'd recognized William standing across the street. Obviously, he'd had something to do with Todd's accident. But what? And why hadn't he called her to tell her he was coming out today?

Celine clicked her nails together so hard she chipped the polish. Who did he think he was, anyway? And why didn't she tell him to get out of her life? Why did she jump every time he said "frog"?

William White was arrogant and cruel, but he was the most incredibly handsome man she'd ever met. She couldn't help it. She was crazy about William. Or maybe she was just crazy, period. As crazy as he was. Women like Celine were supposed to use men, not let men use them

Celine pulled out her compact and began to powder the porcelain-finish makeup that she wore. It was time to demand some explanations. Time to get some kind of commitment.

After all, he was the one who had gotten her

into so much trouble. Because of him and his stupid secret society, Celine had wound up on academic probation and sentenced to all kinds of campus service: Slinging hash in the cafeteria. Filing in the admissions office. Mopping floors in the health center. And starting this afternoon, she was going to be working in the library, re-shelving books. Celine hated the library.

She blew out her breath in a gesture of dis-taste. Good grief. If her granny had any idea that this crappy school was making her precious Celine work like some kind of hired help and waste her youth and good looks hanging around in the library, she'd sure give that Dean Shreeve an earful.

On the other hand, her granny wouldn't have been thrilled with Celine if she'd known that the campus and the DA could have charged Celine with conspiracy to kidnap and commit murder—even though it had been Celine who had ultimately saved Elizabeth's life.

A little shiver of fear ran up Celine's spine. Murder! Would William really have murdered Elizabeth that night at the Sigma house? He had certainly looked capable of murder that night. But was he still?

Celine shut her compact with a brisk snap and glared out the window. William had told her not to call him at the asylum. But she was going to call him anyway. And she was going to keep calling him until she got some answers.

"My steak was great," Tom said. "But I think you made the best choice. Next time I'll get the shrimp."

There was no comment from Jessica, and she stared glumly out the window. A bag with Elizabeth's uneaten lunch sat balanced on her lap.

"Let's take the scenic route," Tom said. He turned the wheel, and they started down a wide boulevard lined with trees. It was a cheerful block with lots of restored Victorian houses. "I like looking at old architecture. How about you?"

"I guess," Jessica responded without interest.

Tom bit his lip in frustration. Elizabeth's parting instructions to him had been to finish brunch and do his best to cheer Jessica up. He was trying hard, but the scene at brunch had really brought her down.

There was a small park at the corner. A mob of little kids ran and jumped and chased one another happily over the grass. Tom pulled the car over. It was hard to stay depressed when you were watching kids play.

"Why are we stopping?" Jessica asked.

31

"It's a gorgeous day," Tom responded. "Let's walk off a few calories and watch the kids."

Jessica nodded and climbed out of the car. Tom removed his blazer, draped it over the back of the seat, and locked the car. "Ahh," he said, turning his face up toward the sun. "It's nice to stretch—" He broke off with a surprised yell as a football hit him squarely between the shoulder blades.

Jessica burst into sputtering laughter, and Tom whirled around to face a group of six boys who looked about nine years old.

"Sorry, mister," one of them said. "Sean did it. He's our kicker, but he's not too good yet."

A tall redheaded boy, who was obviously Sean, began to blush. "Sorry," he muttered. "I've been practicing but . . ." He trailed off and stared at his feet.

"No problem," Tom answered. "And keep practicing. Kicking is almost as hard as passing. But if you practice . . ." He leaned over and picked up the football and then fell back, running as he brought his arm up.

Even in loafers he could feel his muscles and tendons springing to life. And when the football left his hands, it felt so right, so familiar, and so natural he almost cried.

It went sailing through the air in a straight

line toward Sean, who caught the pass with a whoop of joy. The crowd of boys thundered off, and Jessica began to laugh. "Something tells me Tom Watts is not completely finished with the football. Admit it. You miss it, don't you?"

Tom pressed his lips together and didn't answer. She was joking, but she had struck a nerve. "Maybe," he said finally. "A little."

"So why do you always act like you're not interested in sports anymore?"

Tom shrugged. "I'm not, really. What I miss is the . . . *physicality* of football. There's no other sport to match it. And I guess I miss the competition, too."

"What's wrong with that? Why act like it's such a big secret?"

"It's hard to talk to Elizabeth about it," Tom admitted.

It was Jessica's turn to look surprised. "I thought you and Elizabeth could talk about anything."

"Almost anything," Tom said, trying hard not to start feeling defensive. "I don't blame Elizabeth for being down on the athletes around campus. There have been a lot of scandals, and there are some real bad apples—as you found out."

Jessica's cheeks began to turn red.

"I'm sorry. I'm not trying to embarrass you. I know that college athletics and athletes have a reputation for being crooked and thinking the rules don't apply to them. But there are some really great guys who are athletes. I hope you meet some of them. Elizabeth, too."

Jessica smiled a tight smile. "She already has."

"Who?"

"You, dummy!"

Tom grinned and laughed. "Oh, yeah. Right. But I'm not really an athlete anymore." He noticed that her attention seemed to wander and figured she had had enough walking. "Ready to go back to the car?"

"Sure," Jessica answered in a slightly distracted voice.

Jessica felt Tom's hand on her arm, nudging her in the direction of the car. She moved to follow him, but her attention was focused on the figure sitting on the park bench across the street.

Whoever it was seemed to sense that she was staring. He quickly stood and began striding away.

He was tall and, from a distance, very good-looking.

To her surprise, she realized that her heart

was racing. But was it excitement? Or fear? Fear of picking the wrong man yet again.

Jessica yearned to get a closer look at his face. But the sun was shining in her eyes now, and all she could see was a dark silhouette.

"I'm telling you, I was framed!"

Alexandra heard a second voice. A policeman's voice, low and rumbling. But she couldn't make out the words.

She and Elizabeth sat on a bench in the downtown police precinct. There were several police officers and plainclothes detectives wandering in and out.

Temporary holding cells and interrogation rooms were located down the hall, and the girls had heard Todd ranting and raving from the moment they'd arrived.

Alexandra swallowed, fighting tears. It was hard to believe any of this was real. At this time last year, she and Elizabeth had been sure they'd be best friends forever. And Elizabeth and Todd had seemed as though they were destined to be together. Now everything—and everyone—had changed.

"Thanks for coming with me," Elizabeth said suddenly.

"You're welcome," Alexandra answered.

Elizabeth didn't say anything else, and Alexandra racked her brains for something to talk about. Some topic of conversation that wouldn't lead them back to the painful past or the even more painful present.

Both girls jumped and instinctively clutched each other's arms as another enraged bellow emanated from the hallway.

"I didn't steal the car!" Todd screamed. The hysteria in his voice was frightening.

"Ms. Wakefield?"

Alexandra felt Elizabeth's hand relax its grip on her upper arm, and both girls turned their heads toward a man in a business suit with a sheaf of papers in his hand.

"I'm Elizabeth Wakefield," Elizabeth said quietly.

The man cleared his throat. "I'm Louis Tracy, Mr. Wilkins's court-appointed attorney. I understand you're willing to post bond for Mr. Wilkins?"

Elizabeth nodded her head and reached into her purse. "I'll write a check."

"Are you a relative?"

"A friend," Elizabeth answered.

"You understand that if Mr. Wilkins doesn't appear for his hearing, you will forfeit the bond?"

Elizabeth nodded again, and the lawyer held out the papers for Elizabeth to see. Elizabeth cast her eyes over the first form and let out a long, disappointed sigh. "Uh-oh. I don't have that much money in the bank."

"May I?" Alexandra asked tentatively, nodding at the papers.

Mr. Tracy handed her the papers, and Alexandra's heart thumped when she saw the amount of Todd's bond. She reminded herself that she would get it back—eventually—assuming Todd didn't skip town.

But Todd would never skip town. Alexandra put her hand on Elizabeth's sleeve and drew her slightly away. "Why don't I write a check for half and you write a check for half?" she suggested.

Elizabeth's eyes widened. "You'd do that for Todd?"

Alexandra nodded. "Will he be able to leave right away?" she asked the man. "Or will you keep him here until he's sober?"

"He's not drunk," Mr. Tracy replied, sounding as if he was a little surprised about it.

"I've never stolen anything in my life, dammit! I'm telling you it was the guy in the coffee shop."

Mr. Tracy shook his head. "Most people that

37

worked up, it's the alcohol or something." He gave the girls a quizzical look. "Your friend have any kind of history of mental problems?"

Alexandra waited for Elizabeth to deny it. But much to her surprise, Elizabeth said nothing. "Who should this check be made out to?" she asked quietly.

Five minutes later, and substantially poorer, the two girls left the station.

"That was my tuition money," Elizabeth said after a long moment.

"Mine, too," Alexandra said. "But don't worry. We'll get it back."

Elizabeth frowned. "He sounds so crazy. I don't know what to do for him and . . ."

Alexandra put her hand on Elizabeth's shoulder. "Look. You've . . . *we've* . . . done everything for Todd we can do at this point. What we need to do now is leave him alone."

"I'd be happy to leave him alone," Elizabeth said immediately. "But he won't leave me alone."

"What do you mean?"

"I mean, he's doing all these weird things," Elizabeth blurted out. "I guess to get my attention. But it's slightly sick, and it just makes me wonder if . . ."

"If?"

"Like today," Elizabeth said. "I thought maybe he was acting so nutty because he was drunk. But he's not drunk. So maybe he's got problems that go deeper than that."

"You mean like . . . *mental problems?*"

Elizabeth nodded sadly. "You wouldn't believe some of the stuff he's been doing. He's left me some notes that are . . . well . . . strange."

"How do you know it's Todd?"

"Who else would it be?" Elizabeth asked simply.

Alexandra felt a deep sense of unease. She wanted to get away from Todd and the police station. She wanted to get back to Noah's reassuringly normal presence.

Chapter Three

"Come on, man, you can do better than that."

Tom ground his teeth, and his lip lifted in a snarl as he fought the fifty-pound weight on the downward motion of the curl. When the weight was lowered, he released his grip and dropped the weight on the floor. It made a dull thud. Tom whipped the towel from around his neck and mopped his forehead. He gave Danny a grin. "No, I can't. Thirty reps is it. And if that's not good enough for you, then . . ."

Danny's handsome, African-American face broke into a broad smile, and he held up his hand. "Whoaaa! Thirty reps is plenty good enough for me. Good enough for anybody—except you."

Tom lifted his face from the towel. "Huh?"

His best friend straddled the desk chair and folded his arms across the back. "What I mean, my friend, is the only one who never thinks Tom Watts is good enough is Tom Watts. Be honest. You were shooting for forty, weren't you?"

Sometimes Danny was a little too insightful, Tom decided. "If you've developed a talent for mind reading, you're going to have to find a new best friend. I need privacy—at least between my ears."

Danny's face fell a fraction. "I didn't mean to get intrusive."

Tom mopped his forehead again. "Sorry, man. It's just that you're the second person to hit that nerve."

"What's the problem?"

"I feel like I'm falling short."

"You're on the dean's list," Danny reminded him. "You're the star broadcast journalist and the principal force behind the campus television station. And you're dating a girl who would rate twenty on a scale of one to ten. In what sense, exactly, do you feel like you're falling short?"

Tom surveyed the collection of free weights that littered the floor of the dorm room he and Danny shared. "Physically. I mean, I lift weights. I run. But I can't seem to get enough exercise—at least, I'm not getting any satisfaction from my workouts."

"Maybe because you do all those things by yourself. I think you miss contact—literally and figuratively. You miss the physical outlet a contact sport provides, and you miss communicating with the other players. You need to be part of a team."

"Go ahead, say it," Tom urged.

Danny walked over to his own desk and began loading books into his backpack. "I think you should seriously consider getting back on the football team."

Tom shook his head. "No way."

"Why not?"

"I can't," Tom whispered. "I couldn't handle it before—my ego just got totally out of control."

Danny shrugged. "That was then. This is now. You're older. You're wiser. And you're making me late." He looked at his watch. "I gotta go. I'm meeting Isabella at the cafeteria for breakfast. Then we're hitting the library."

Tom picked up one of the smaller weights and moodily executed another few curls. "I'll see you later, then."

Danny slung his backpack over one shoulder,

grabbed his jacket from the bed, and lifted his hand in a wave. "Later."

The door closed, and Tom fell back on his bed with a loud sigh. Football!

I thought you and Elizabeth could talk about anything, Jessica had said.

Elizabeth was a very understanding woman. But after the recruiting scandals that had rocked the basketball team, her opinion of college athletics had gone downhill. And James Montgomery's sexual assault on her sister hadn't done anything to help.

The phone rang, and Tom got up and stepped over the weight, answering it before the second ring. "Hello?"

"Tom Watts?" a friendly voice inquired.

"Speaking."

"Tom, my name is Bob, and I'm a freelance producer trying to put together a package of pieces for VideoNet News Services. I was in Sweet Valley a while back and caught some of your work on the public-access channel down there. You're a good reporter."

Tom felt a little breathless. "Thank you. Thanks a lot. That means a lot coming from a professional producer."

Bob chuckled. "Listen, I've been kicking around an idea for a sports story for a while, and

I think you might be the reporter to handle it. Would you be interested in doing a piece that has the potential to be aired on national news?"

Tom's heart turned over. He could hardly believe what he was hearing. It sounded as though he was about to be offered a shot at the professional news market. "Of course," he managed to choke. "What did you have in mind?"

"As you probably know, Tom, college sports scandals aren't happening just at SVU—they're a national problem. I did a little checking up on your background, and I was amazed at what I found out. You were an up-and-coming football star. What happened?"

"Nothing related to a scandal," Tom said quickly. "It was a personal decision. That's all."

"Could you tell me a little bit about it?"

Tom hesitated. Talking about personal problems with a stranger wasn't something he would typically do.

"Tom, I'm not asking because I'm nosy. I'm asking because your credibility is what's going to help me sell this story to the network bigwigs."

"My parents were killed on the way to a game," Tom said quickly. "I haven't played since."

There was a long pause on the other end of

the line. Finally, Bob let out a long sigh. "I'm really sorry about that, Tom. I had no idea."

"That's OK," Tom said, hoping they could move on to the specifics of the assignment.

"Under the circumstances, I'm not sure how you're going to feel about what I'm about to propose, but I'll run it by you anyway."

"I'm all ears," Tom replied.

"I want somebody to get inside the story of a team coming back after a scandal. The James Montgomery story has been all over the sports-news industry, and something like that's got to have an impact on the way a team feels about itself and how it functions. The SVU-versus-State game is coming up soon. Now, I know this is a wild idea, but keep an open mind. What if you could sub for James Montgomery at that game?"

"What?"

"Sub for James Montgomery. He's off the team, and he was their star. You've got all the moves he's got. In fact, from what I've heard, you're better than he is."

"*Was* better," Tom corrected.

"So start shaping up now. Call Coach Barker. See if he's interested. If he is, put on the jersey. Go to the practices. Talk to the guys. Find out what happens in the aftermath of a scandal. And needless to say, keep quiet about what you're doing. You want people to be candid with you. You want them to open up. I think it would be a hell of a piece of investigative reporting. What do you think?"

Tom realized his head was nodding up and down. The guy was right. It was a great idea for a story. "I'll do it."

"Great. Listen, I'll be in Europe for a few weeks, and I'll be pretty much unreachable. But you go ahead and get the ball rolling. I'll be doing what I can to sell this story, and I'll catch up with you before the game. If I can sell the piece, the pay is union scale plus five percent. Fair enough?"

"Fine by me." Tom had no idea how much union scale was, but getting paid anything at all was going to be a thrill.

There was a deep chuckle on the other end of the line. "Welcome to the pros, Tom."

"Thanks a lot. And good-bye." Tom replaced the receiver, almost in a daze. He felt like Cinderella or something. This was an incredible opportunity. He picked up the receiver and punched the keypad.

"Campus information. May I help you?"

"Yes. Could you please give me the extension for the football office?"

*   *   *

"Knife!" Denise Waters barked, holding her hand out.

"Knife," Winston Egbert repeated, slapping a dull stainless-steel knife into her hand.

"Cream cheese," Denise said.

"Cream cheese." Winston handed her a dish of softened cream cheese.

"Lox," Denise demanded.

"Lox? On my allowance? You've got to be kidding."

Denise giggled and began spreading the two halves of the bagel she and Winston were sharing with cream cheese. "Who needs lox when you have love?"

Love! Winston's heart gave a strange thud, and he searched Denise's beautiful face for a clue as to whether or not she was joking. Winston loved Denise with all his heart—and he had from the very first moment he laid eyes on her.

Denise, he knew, was crazy about him, but it was hard to get her to take him seriously. In fact, he reflected, it was hard to get anyone to take him seriously. That was the downside of being the class-clown type.

Oh, sure, clowns got the laughs. But did they ever get the girl?

Winston and Denise were sitting in Winston's room, with the school newspaper spread out on the floor, two cups of steaming coffee from the cafeteria take-out, and bagels from the gourmet bakery that was located in the basement of the student union.

Denise was doing the honors, because after breaking his arm, Winston was still wearing a lightweight cast on his forearm.

The cast was really unnecessary at this point, but Denise had been making a fond and sympathetic fuss over him, and he didn't want it to stop. "What do you want to do tonight?" Winston asked.

Denise shrugged. "Where's the entertainment section?"

"Behind you." Winston started to reach, but Denise lightly pushed him back to his sitting position.

"Don't strain your arm," she said. "Hold this." She handed him her half of the bagel.

Then, in front of his amazed eyes, she rolled backward until her body was in the shape of a U, her legs and upper torso perfectly parallel with the floor. With a deft motion, she gripped the paper between two of her toes and then rolled her legs over until she was sitting up again.

"Hold mine now," Winston said, unable to resist a chance to show off.

Denise took his bagel and Winston quickly rolled backward, configuring his body in the same shape as Denise's. Then he lifted his legs and straightened his back until he was balancing on his head. He pressed down with his hands and lifted his body until he was standing on his hands. Finally, he curved his body backward, planted his feet, and gracefully stood up, before taking a deep bow.

Denise stared at him with an open mouth. "I didn't know you could do that," she gasped. "You took tumbling, didn't you?"

"Only a couple of semesters," he answered. "In middle school."

Denise's face darkened. "And while we're on the subject, how did you manage to do that with your bad arm?"

Winston felt the color rush to his face. "Ummmmm . . ."

"Winston!" Denise glowered. "Have you been pretending to be helpless just to get attention?"

Winston grinned. "Well, why not? Girls do it all the time. Act helpless so they'll bring out men's protective instincts."

"I hope your instincts for *self*-protection are pretty strong right now," she growled, "because

50

you're going to need them." She picked up the dull knife and pretended to lunge.

Winston jumped backward with his hands in the air. "Please let me live!" he shrieked.

Denise collapsed on the floor in giggles. She lifted her face, and he leaned forward to kiss her. Suddenly, a headline in the newspaper caught his eye.

He veered sideways, grabbing for the paper. "Look at this," he said. "They're looking for a new Braino." He held the paper and moved slightly so she could read along with him.

Braino was an SVU tradition. A clown who was both a mascot and a cheerleader. The Braino mask covered the head and came down over the eyes and nose. A mortarboard and tassel were precariously perched on top of a mop of carrot-colored curls.

Braino heads were always on sale at the bookstore, since lots of people liked to wear them to games. Winston had bought one the day he arrived on campus.

According to the article, Mark Janos, a very funny senior who had been Braino for the past two years, was taking a short leave of absence to have foot surgery.

"Winston!" Denise cried. "You should try out. You'd be perfect."

Winston grinned. "It would be fun, wouldn't it?"

"Yes. And just think, you'd get to drive the Brainmobile to all the away games."

Winston began to laugh. The Brainmobile was a four-door sedan painted with the school colors and covered with pennants and stickers.

Traditionally, the Brainmobile followed the charter buses that transported the team and the students to away games. Along the way—at rest stops and on the road—Braino did impromptu routines. Tumbling. Magic. Balloon tricks.

"I don't think so," Winston said.

"Why not?" Denise demanded.

"Mark Janos is a great gymnast. No way could I do all that stuff he did."

"So we'll practice," Denise said decisively. "You can do it, Winston. And I think you should."

She grabbed his hand and pulled him to a standing position. "Look at you. You're a perfect Braino. Tall. Limber. Funny-looking . . ."

"Funny-looking!"

"Funny as in ha ha, make you laugh. Not funny as in strange or geeky."

"I don't want to be ha ha funny-looking," Winston croaked. "I don't want women to look at me and laugh. I want women to look at me and swoon."

"Yeah! And I'd like men to look at me and run screaming in fear. But we are what we are. You're funny-looking, and I love it." She stood on tiptoe and pecked the end of Winston's nose again.

Love. There. She'd said it twice now. But did she mean it? "Denise," he began in a husky voice.

"We'll start with some stretching exercises," she said. "Flop over like this. Her upper torso drooped forward, and she let her arms fall toward the floor as she swayed back and forth.

"One . . . two . . . one . . . two . . . *Winston!*"

"I'm flopping. I'm flopping." If being the campus clown would impress Denise, he wasn't about to miss his chance.

William rolled toward the University Center in the wheelchair he'd bought from a secondhand shop. Kimberly Schyler and Tina Meyer both passed him—looked right at his face and then passed by without a flicker of recognition.

It was amazing how body language and posture could provide such a complete disguise. William White had been a personage on the

SVU campus. A face known to every student and every faculty member. Yet, he'd been hanging around on campus for weeks now without being recognized. All he had to do was slump his shoulders, throw on a wig, and sit in the wheelchair.

Tom Watts came striding out the front doors of the University Center with a paper under one arm. William lifted his face slightly, letting Tom get a good look at it. It was a risk—but men like William weren't afraid to take risks.

Tom came closer, and William felt Tom's eyes rest on his face . . . His heart stopped for a slight moment and then resumed its calm beating as Tom went on past him, never breaking his long stride.

It was all William could do not to laugh. What an inferior intellect. What an inferior person in every sense. Even the stupidest of dogs sensed danger when it came so near.

William swallowed his laughter and kept rolling along the sidewalk and up the ramp. A pretty freshman held the front door of the University Center open for him, and he smiled his thanks. When the door closed behind him, he rolled down the hall until he reached the newspaper rack that stood outside the entrance to the cafeteria.

He took one and scanned the headlines. A new degree plan was being introduced in the Anthropology department. A record number of parking tickets had been issued in the last month. All students were cautioned that there would be a penalty of five dollars levied for bounced checks to the bookstore.

On page three, he found what he was looking for. He smiled. The two stories were side by side.

In the left-hand column, there was a short, two-paragraph announcement that Todd Wilkins had been suspended from SVU because of felony charges filed over the weekend.

And in the right-hand column, there was a short two-paragraph announcement that Tom Watts had rejoined the football team.

Elizabeth lifted her fist and banged on the door.

"Come in," she heard Tom call out.

Elizabeth pushed the door open and walked in. He was sitting at his desk, leaning over a book. He smiled when he lifted his head. But when he saw her face, his smile disappeared and a wary expression took its place. "You saw the paper."

"Yeah. I saw the paper." She was so furious, her hands were shaking. "How come I have to read something like this in the paper? Why didn't you tell me what you were planning to do?"

Tom closed his book and cleared his throat. "Liz, I love you, but . . ."

"But you don't trust me enough to take me into your confidence," she finished for him. She was angry, and she was bewildered. "Don't you realize how excluded from your life this makes me feel?"

"Look! I had to make a decision. I know you have strong feelings about sports and . . ."

"What I have are strong feelings about *you*," she choked.

"I have strong feelings about you, too," he countered, his voice rising. "But that doesn't mean I'm going to discuss all my plans with you. I'm a grown man," he snapped. "And I'm going to run my own life."

"Who's trying to run your life?"

"You are."

"I am *not*."

"Then why are you so mad that I've done something you don't approve of?"

Elizabeth opened and closed her mouth. How could he be so incredibly obtuse?

All she'd heard for weeks now was how painful the whole subject of football and his past stardom had been. And then suddenly, out of nowhere, he had signed back onto the team.

She stared at his face, which was studiously blank. There was no use trying to talk to him. Abruptly, she turned on her heel and marched toward the door.

"Where are you going?"

She whirled. "I'm a grown woman. I don't have to discuss all my plans with you." She stormed out, slamming the door shut behind her.

The heels of her boots made a fierce drumming sound on the pavement as she left Tom's dorm and headed across the quad walkway toward her dorm. She bit down on her lower lip, determined not to cry.

When she reached Dickenson Hall, she hurried up the stairs and down the hall to her room. She opened her door and clasped her hand over her mouth to muffle a scream. Then she backed up, closed the door to her room, and stood perfectly still. Someone had been in her room. Was he still there?

She listened for several seconds but heard no sound. Cautiously, she opened the door and stepped inside again. She moved closer to the bed.

Lying on her bed were a Barbie doll and a Ken doll. A red gash was painted across Ken's throat. Barbie's hands were thrown upward, and her mouth had been painted over so that it formed the shape of an "O"—as if she were screaming.

Elizabeth sat down on the bed, pretty firmly convinced now that the prankster was Todd.

Your friend have any kind of history of mental problems?

She remembered the irrational way Todd had been screaming in the police station. He was going over the edge. But was he dangerous?

Should she tell Tom?

Elizabeth immediately rejected that idea. If Tom was determined to work through his problems without her, she could work through her problems without him.

Todd was going through some bad times. The notes. The dolls. They were bids for attention and pleas for help. But he needed to get that attention and help from someone other than Elizabeth. And he needed to hear that from Elizabeth's own mouth.

She took the stairs again, trotting briskly toward the front door. On her way out, she dumped the dolls in a trash can.

Elizabeth circled around the building and began walking across campus toward Marsden Hall, the athletic dorm where Todd lived.

She knocked softly at the door and heard footsteps cross the room. The door opened slightly, and Todd's face peered out. "Elizabeth!" he exclaimed.

"I need to talk to you."

Todd's eyes darted past her, trying to see around the door. "Are you alone?"

"Yes, of course."

Todd hesitated a moment, then backed up and opened the door wide enough to let her in.

Elizabeth felt momentarily frightened. But she relaxed when she saw the look on Todd's face. There was no violent emotion there—just empty resignation.

There were piles of clothes all around. He motioned to her to sit and then began removing sweaters from a drawer and placing them in a large suitcase. "Thanks for posting my bail," he said.

"Alexandra put up half of it."

Todd smoothed his hand over the sweaters. "Thank her for me, will you? Somehow, I don't think she'd want to hear from me directly." He began removing his textbooks from the bookshelf and piling them into a cardboard carton.

Elizabeth watched his back. He looked tired and defeated, but he didn't look nuts. "I want to talk to you about what's been going on."

"I didn't steal the car," Todd stated.

"I'm not talking about the car. I'm talking about the stuff you left in my room."

Todd turned and lifted his brows. "What stuff?"

"The dolls."

"The dolls?" he repeated in a bewildered tone.

"Todd!" Elizabeth insisted. "I know it's you. And I want it to stop."

Todd shook his head, and then took a deep breath. "Elizabeth. I'm really, really confused right now. About a lot of things. And you're not helping." He looked at his watch. "Listen. The RA says I've got to be out of here in an hour, so if you don't mind . . ."

He opened the door, obviously inviting her to leave, but Elizabeth stayed put and crossed her arms over her chest. "Where are you going?"

"Believe it or not, the guy who owns the bar on the corner of Elm and Seventh called me. He's got a room over the bar he'll let me use in exchange for some work in the bar." He shrugged. "Turns out he's a big sports fan."

Elizabeth felt her anger turning into pity. She couldn't imagine Todd mopping floors and washing beer mugs in some scuzzy bar. "Todd! Why don't you just go home? You could ask your parents for help, and then come back and make a fresh start next semester."

Todd shook his head. "No way can I tell my parents. My getting kicked off the team practically killed them. Besides, the police told me not to leave the area." He gave her a small smile. "Don't forget—if I skip town, you're out a big chunk of money." He took her arm and gently propelled her toward the door.

"I won't let you down, Elizabeth," he said with quiet dignity. "I'll be at the hearing." Then the door shut quietly in her face.

Chapter Four

"Yuck!" Jessica stuck her tongue out at her own reflection and then made a disgusted face. "Look at the dark circles under my eyes."

"Don't be silly," Elizabeth said, squeezing in beside her at the sink. "You look great."

Jessica reached into her huge makeup bag and fished around in it for concealer. "Actually, they're not as bad as they were last week." She giggled. "Hey. Maybe I've stumbled onto a new beauty secret—football. Last Saturday was the best night's sleep I've had in weeks."

Elizabeth had been delighted when Jessica had returned from brunch last Saturday in such a good mood. But right now she considered football a sore subject. She couldn't help grimacing as she squirted toothpaste onto her toothbrush.

"Why are you scowling?" Jessica asked.

"Did you see the paper yesterday?"

"No."

"Tom rejoined the football team."

Jessica set down her concealer and turned to Elizabeth. "Are you kidding me?"

Elizabeth shook her head. "Nope. He's taking over James's spot." She jammed the toothbrush into her mouth and began to brush furiously.

"Take it easy," Jessica cautioned. "You're going to brush your teeth away if you keep that up."

Elizabeth spat angrily into the sink and then turned on the water full blast. "I'm just really hurt that he didn't talk to me about it first," she said, pulling a towel off the rack and patting her face. "Obviously, it's been on his mind for a long time."

"Maybe," Jessica said. "Maybe not. Tom talked to me a little bit about it and . . ."

"Tom talked to *you*?" Elizabeth cried. "Oh, great. He shares more with my sister than with me." She yanked open the bathroom door and stomped out.

Jessica grabbed her cosmetics bag and hurried after her. "I don't mean he asked for my advice or anything. But he did say it was hard for him to talk to you about football."

Elizabeth whirled around. "That's because *he's* the one who's always telling me it's a painful subject."

"That's probably so," Jessica answered. "But he also cares a whole lot about what you think—and he doesn't think you have too great an opinion of athletes."

"Does he really believe I'm so judgmental that I think nobody should ever play a sport because some guys on the team are jerks?"

"No. He thinks you're wonderful, and he doesn't want to do anything to upset you."

"Then why did he join the football team?"

"So you *are* upset that he joined?"

Elizabeth reached back and tightened her ponytail. "Yes. No. I don't know. I mean, if that's what he wants to do, then I want to support that decision. But how can I be supportive if he won't talk to me about what he's thinking?"

"Maybe you should ask him that question. Why don't you call him?"

Elizabeth slung her towel over her shoulder and resumed her long strides down the hall toward their room. "Forget it. If he wants to straighten this out, he knows where to find me."

Jessica ducked into the bathroom for one

last look in the mirror, then followed Elizabeth down the hall. She wasn't going to have much time to deliberate over her wardrobe this morning.

Elizabeth pushed the door of their room open and skidded to a halt so suddenly that Jessica banged her nose on the back of Elizabeth's head. "Ouch!" she protested. "Did you really have to test your brakes now?"

She waited for Elizabeth to laugh, but her sister made no sound. "Liz?" Jessica's gaze followed Elizabeth's, and she suddenly felt her stomach lurch. "Oh, gross!" she said, choking and pressing her hand over her mouth.

"This is sick," Elizabeth said through gritted teeth. "This is unbelievably sick. It's evil."

Jessica walked over to Elizabeth's bed and stared at the awful tableau. When she glanced over at her own bed, her eyes widened with fear. They were dressed just alike. Two Barbie dolls with long blond hair dressed in pink formals. Both dolls were splattered with red paint and lay with their arms and legs twisted and broken.

"That's it!" Elizabeth said, slamming the door and stalking over to the bed. "I can't take it anymore. I can't believe I was stupid enough to bail him out of jail just so he could harass

66

me." She threw both Barbie dolls into the wastebasket and then wrapped her arm around Jessica.

Jessica raised her eyebrows. "You think *Todd* did this?"

"Don't you?"

"This doesn't seem like something Todd would do," Jessica said. "I mean . . . *Todd*? He's Mr. . . ."

"He's Mr. Weird these days," Elizabeth finished angrily, removing her arm from around Jessica's shoulders. "Look, Alex and I had a long talk on the way back from the police station. She told me that aside from drinking, Todd's been losing his temper, doing all kinds of things that you wouldn't expect. And who else could it be?"

"William White," Jessica answered grimly.

"William White is in an institution for the criminally insane," Elizabeth snapped.

"Maybe."

"What do you mean, maybe?" Elizabeth's face was pale, and her eyes looked unusually large and round. Jessica knew her twin's worst fear was that some nitwit psychiatrist would decide William was mentally competent and turn him loose.

Jessica took Elizabeth's hand. "Look. I know the idea of William's being loose is almost more than you can handle. But I think you should call that place and double-check."

"It's not William White. It's Todd," Elizabeth insisted. "Why are you trying to make me think it could be William?"

"Because no matter how bent Todd's brain is right now, I can't see him doing something like this."

Elizabeth sat down in her desk chair. "I don't know what to think about Todd anymore. But I do know I'd rather have Todd stalking me than William White."

"Then let's make sure it's not William," Jessica urged. "Go on. Call."

Elizabeth chewed her bottom lip. Then she abruptly reached for the phone book and flipped the pages until she found the name of the institution. She reached for the phone.

Jessica lowered her head so she could listen to the receiver with Elizabeth.

A female voice answered on the second ring. "Patient Information."

Elizabeth hesitated for a moment, uncertain of what to say.

"Hello?" The voice sounded slightly irritated now.

"Oh, yes, hello," Elizabeth sputtered. "I was just calling to . . . to . . ."

". . . check on a patient. William White," Jessica filled in.

"I'm sorry, Mr. White cannot come to the phone."

"But he is there?" Jessica pressed.

"He can't come to the phone," the voice repeated. "But I'm allowed to take messages for him. Would you like to leave your name?"

"No!" Elizabeth said quickly, pulling away from Jessica. "I'll call back some other time." She slammed the phone down. "There," she said, giving Jessica a thin smile. "Satisfied?"

Jessica noticed that Elizabeth's hands were shaking. "Are you?"

Elizabeth nodded. "Yeah. I'm glad you made me call. Todd I can handle. But William . . ." She didn't have to finish her thought. If a monster like William was after Jessica, Jessica knew she wouldn't be able to handle it, either.

Andrea stood with her hand resting on the telephone receiver. William had told her to expect calls from terrorist enemies seeking information about his movements. And he had cautioned her to say nothing except that he was a patient at the institution and that she could take messages.

Poor William. He was under so much pressure.

Fighting so hard to keep the world free from the forces of oppression and evil. It made her want to protect him—which is why she hadn't bothered him by passing on the messages he'd gotten over the last few days.

She sat down and moodily twirled her hair around her index finger. William had received several phone calls from the same woman. Celine. Was she really a terrorist enemy?

Andrea swiveled back and forth in the desk chair, jealousy and doubt beginning to make her heart drum faster. She stood and pulled the handful of pink message slips from the pocket of her lab coat. One by one, she dropped them into the trash can.

Celine dropped a load of books into the wooden library cart and started toward the elevator. She pushed the button and then tapped the toe of her high-heel pump in anger and frustration. What was William up to? Why hadn't he returned any of her calls?

Celine wasn't used to men not calling her back. Sure, it probably wasn't too easy to call from a maximum-security loony bin, but William always managed to do whatever he wanted. If he had wanted to call Celine, he would have found a way.

The elevator arrived, and Celine gave the cart a hard push. Why didn't he contact her? Why? It had been so long. Too long. As the door closed, she groaned. William was like an addiction. An addiction to an exhilarating, exciting, and unpredictable drug.

The doors opened, and Celine let out a long sigh of boredom. She still couldn't believe that the school actually had the authority to force her to work for nothing at the most boring task in the whole world—shelving books in the basement stacks.

The small round wheels of the wooden cart squeaked slightly as she made her way through the narrow passages that wound into the deepest recesses of the library basement.

She paused at a shelf and glared at the books that had been stacked carelessly on the wrong shelf. It didn't matter what jackass put things in the wrong place, the head librarian always blamed Celine. Like it or not, she was going to have to clear the shelf and rearrange everything. She grabbed the spines of four books at once and pulled them off the shelf. She gasped when she found herself staring right into a familiar pair of icy blue eyes.

She blinked, hardly daring to believe he was real. In that instant, the face on the other side of the shelf disappeared. The next thing Celine heard was the echo of footsteps.

"William!" she cried, dropping the books on the floor. "William, wait!" Her high heels clattered on the floor as she ran into the old manuscript and map room. She shivered—the place was like a mausoleum. "William. It's me. Celine."

She paused for a moment, panting, straining her ears. Far away, she thought she heard the sound of someone running. Then she heard the creak of a door, and a slam.

She hurried to the very back room of the library and paused outside the door that said DO NOT ENTER. She wrenched the door open and stepped into the hall.

The door shut behind her with a bang, sealing her off from the rest of the library. The only noise was the dull and steady roar of machinery. And except for the dim glare that emanated from a fluorescent tube mounted on the low ceiling, there was no light.

"William?" she whispered. "Where are you?"

A slight sound from behind a tall piece of machinery drew her attention. "William. Why don't you answer me?"

There was a strange sound, low and deep.

"William? Are you *laughing*?"

The laughter began to boom now, filling the narrow passageway.

Her heart began to hammer when William stepped out from a dark shadow.

Celine felt half-delirious with delight, but half-sick with fear. William was insane. If he didn't want Celine to find him, maybe she'd made a terrible mistake in coming to look for him. "William?" she began in a small, trembling voice. "Please don't be angry. It's just that I've been wanting to see you and . . ."

"I'm glad you followed me," he said finally.

She felt a sense of relief. He wasn't angry. He was glad she had followed him. Glad to see her. She rushed forward, stretching her arms toward him. "I knew it. . . ."

But William deflected her caress by grabbing her wrists and pulling her arms to her sides. "I need you to do something for me."

"Anything," she said.

His lips curved into a seductive smile, and Celine felt her body respond. His eyes were cold, but there was passion in his grip.

"My wheelchair is on the third floor behind the periodicals. Get rid of it for me, will you?"

Celine felt her face fall. "That's it?"

William released her wrists. "That's it," he said, beginning to back into the shadows.

73

"But . . . William. What does this mean? Are you leaving?"

"Just get rid of the wheelchair," he repeated.

"William!" she cried. "William, what are you up to? Does this mean you're leaving Sweet Valley?"

"You know how I feel about questions," he reminded her.

"But I have to know." Celine rushed toward him, determined to find out what his plans were.

William reached up and smashed his fist into the light fixture. There was a splattering, sizzling sound and a shower of sparks, before the hallway was plunged into darkness. "William!" she screamed. "Please, don't leave me here! I don't know how to get out!"

The only answer was the sound of his footsteps disappearing into the distance. She was alone and disoriented in the pitch-black dark.

Panic rose in Celine's throat, and she fought the impulse to begin screaming hysterically. Where was the doorway? How did she get out?

She was sobbing now and her hands clawed at the cold cinder-block walls. Finally, her hand found the doorway. She groped for the handle, wrenched the door open, and fell to the floor of the back room of the library.

Celine lay on the cold parquet, panting with terror. She was wet with perspiration and sick with disappointment. William White, it appeared, was through with her.

Elizabeth was glad that she'd had a chance to calm down before Tom called. When he'd asked her to meet him at the library, she had managed to keep her voice under control and to sound one hundred percent cool, calm, and collected. She didn't want Tom to know what Todd was up to. He might have a machismo attack and take matters into his own hands.

She looked at her watch. As usual, she was right on time. "Just hopelessly type A," she muttered as she entered the front doors of the library and began searching for Tom.

He was sitting at his usual table. And, as usual, he had about six textbooks, three binders, and twenty index cards spread out around him. A freshly sharpened pencil was stuck behind one ear.

Wordlessly, she sat down across from him and waited. He lifted his head and gave her a rueful smile. "Thanks for meeting me here. I've got to report to practice in twenty minutes, but I really wanted to talk to you."

Elizabeth raised her eyebrows. "I'm listening."

Tom sat back, removed the pencil from behind his ear, and tapped it against the table. "I don't know how to say this."

"What? '*I'm sorry*'?"

"I'm sorry I raised my voice. I'm sorry I was rude. But I'm not sorry that I rejoined the football team."

Elizabeth threw up her arms. "I don't know how to make my feelings any clearer. I'm not mad that you joined the football team. I'm mad that you did a one-hundred-eighty-degree attitude change and I never had a clue it was coming. I thought we knew each other better than that. And I thought you trusted me more than that."

"I do trust you. But I think this is something that you just don't understand."

"So explain it."

"I can't."

"Yes, you can. You're a journalist. If you can't explain something, who can?"

Tom tugged at his earlobe and shifted uncomfortably in his chair. "I miss being on a team. I miss competition. And yeah, when you get right down to it, I miss plowing some two-hundred-and-seventy-pound linebacker into the turf. Sue me. I'm a barbarian."

Elizabeth sat back and stared at him. "Why

76

do I have the feeling you're not being straight with me?"

A red flush deepened Tom's tan, and his face contorted into a scowl. "What do you want from me?"

"Hey! You're the one who arranged this get-together. What do *you* want from *me*?"

Tom held up his hands and winced. "What I want is for us to be OK. I don't want you to be mad at me. I need support right now, not psychological second-guessing." His eyes appealed to her from beneath the thick, dark lashes. "Don't be mad at me," he said. "Please believe that I know what I'm doing." His hand reached across the table. "Please," he repeated more softly.

Elizabeth felt her face and her spine relax. She lifted her own hand and put it on the table. "I won't be mad anymore," she agreed reluctantly.

"Promise?" His hand closed over hers and squeezed.

She gave his hand an answering squeeze and even managed a smile. "I promise," she said softly.

Chapter Five

Celine trudged through the front door of her dingy off campus apartment. All she wanted to do now was throw herself on her bed and have a good old-fashioned bawl.

When her eyes fell on the tattered desk an old tenant had left behind, her breath left her lungs with a loud whooshing sound. Slowly, she approached the desk, hardly able to believe what she was seeing.

Someone had left a Barbie doll with honey-colored curls, a frothy silver dress, and big blue eyes. A Barbie doll that looked like Celine.

The doll leaned against the back wall of the desk in a casual pose—but there was a piece of duct tape across the doll's mouth.

The meaning was clear: "Keep quiet!"

Celine felt an explosion of joy inside her

chest. William wasn't through with her. If he were, he wouldn't have bothered to leave her a message. But why did he feel it necessary to give her such a message? She'd always kept quiet about his comings and goings. Did he suddenly not trust her anymore? And if he didn't, why? She'd certainly done everything she could to reassure him. Written him. Called.

Called!

Celine's eyes narrowed. She'd gotten that same girl every time she'd phoned. The one who was helping him. Andrea, he'd said her name was. She'd sounded like a real dork over the phone.

Why was she helping William? There was only one explanation that Celine could think of. She was in love with him.

"If I were in love with a guy," she asked herself out loud, "would I give him a bunch of messages from another girl? Hell, no."

Celine smiled. A big, broad, Cheshire cat smile. No wonder William didn't trust her. He didn't know she'd called. He'd probably concluded that Celine was no longer on his side.

She ran to the mirror and examined her reflection. She needed a complete redo—foundation, lipstick, eyes, everything. A different outfit, too. Then she was going to drive out to the Harrington

Institution and have a little chat with William—
one on one. It was time to reassure him. Time to
get things straightened out—with him *and* that
Andrea.

"So she does understand now?" Danny asked.

Tom pulled on a fresh T-shirt and grimaced.
He'd spent all afternoon at practice. His coach
had been right. It was all there in his memory
bank—the plays, the signals, the strategies—but
his muscles were really feeling the strain. "She
says she does, but there's a distance."

"What do you mean, a distance?"

Tom opened a drawer and looked through a
pile of sweaters until he found one that was
extra soft. "A distance. You know. A gap. A gulf.
Something we can't seem to bridge. She feels
like I excluded her from the decision-making
process. It came as a big surprise."

"Tell her to join the club," Danny said. "I
don't care if it was in the paper, I wouldn't
have believed it unless I had heard it from you.
I had no idea you'd been nursing this big de-
sire to play football again. No idea at all.
Whenever I suggested it to you, your answer
was a flat *no way*."

Tom turned his back so that Danny couldn't
see the red flush that was making his face feel

81

hot. He hated keeping things from Danny almost as much as he hated keeping things from Elizabeth. But Bob, the producer, had asked him to keep quiet, and Tom wanted to pull this thing off as professionally as possible.

Finally, Tom sat down on the edge of his bed and pulled on his boots. He gave Danny a wide grin and a shrug. "What can I say? Life and Tom Watts are full of surprises."

The door to William's cell opened with a loud bang. "You have a visitor," Andrea informed him coldly.

William sat up slowly. Who was dropping in to visit him? And why was Andrea upset?

"You're not supposed to have drop-in visitors," Andrea continued. "The rules say that all guests must arrange visits at least two weeks ahead of time and make their request in writing."

William stood and walked toward her. "Who's here?" he asked, ignoring her lecture on the rules. "A friend? Or a foe?" he asked softly.

"A girl," she snapped.

Girl? His heart leapt. Was it possible that Elizabeth had intuited his plans for her? Maybe his ever-growing and volcanic passion for her had communicated itself to her via the force of his intellect. Was she ready to join him as his partner in life?

"Her name is Celine," Andrea added sullenly.

The smile that had been forming abruptly left his face. "Celine!"

"And don't tell me she's some kind of operative, or terrorist, because she just looks like a tacky blonde." Andrea seemed to reach a decision and backed out of the door. "I'm going to tell her you can't see her. It's against the rules." She tried to swing the door shut, but William thrust his arm out.

"I have to see her." He really didn't relish the prospect of a wrestling match with a jealous orderly, so he opted for tact and diplomacy. "Andrea," he whispered. "Petty feelings like jealousy have no place in the world of global politics." He squeezed her arm. "Think of your country," he reminded her.

"So she *is* an operative?" Andrea asked in a skeptical tone.

William tugged ruefully at an earlobe. "Now, Andrea, *sweetie*, you know I can't tell you things like that. But suffice it to say her assistance is vital to my . . . er . . . shall we say *continued good health*?"

Andrea's eyes met his, and she clutched protectively at his arm. "Are you in danger?"

It was all William could do not to sneer in her gullible face. How could anyone be so unbelievably, irredeemably stupid?

"Is someone trying to kill you?" she pressed.

"That's what I'm trying to find out," William said in a kind, elaborately patient voice. "Now, will you take me to the visitors' room?"

Andrea shook her head. "Better not. Reed is on duty at the outer desk. I'll bring her into the locked ward. You can meet in one of the offices."

William pulled her to him and planted a passionate kiss on her lips. "Thank you, Andrea, my *angel*."

She smiled and gestured for him to follow her down the hallway. Andrea's crepe-soled shoes made no noise. William walked softly behind her, letting most of his weight fall on the balls of his slippered feet. He didn't want to rouse any of the other inmates.

At last, Andrea opened the door to an office he knew well. "Wait here," she said. "And keep the door closed. I'll bring Celine through the south entrance to the ward."

William blew her a grateful kiss snd sat down in the desk chair. He put his fingers together and thoughtfully swiveled back and forth.

What a nuisance! He'd thought he was through with Celine.

But she clearly wasn't through with him.

Maybe it was better this way. Maybe it was too soon to burn that bridge. Celine might still prove useful.

His mind turned faster and faster as he thought his way through the next several steps of his plan. In a few minutes, the door opened, and Celine stepped inside. "I didn't understand at first," she said.

"What didn't you understand?" William asked, using all his acting ability to infuse some warmth into his voice. Never had he felt as disgusted by Celine's obvious brand of beauty as he did now. He hated her short, tight skirt, her teased curls, her bright pink lips.

"I didn't understand why you were so elusive. You don't trust me, do you?"

"I don't completely trust *anybody*," William answered.

She stepped forward, her eyelashes fluttering and her hands waving in the air. "William, I know I helped get you into this place. But I've done everything you've asked since then, and I've always been on your side. When you didn't call me back, I thought it meant that we were through."

"Call you back?" he asked.

Celine nodded emphatically. "Yes. I've been calling you. Over and over. I told that girl," Celine said darkly.

"I never got any messages," William said quietly. His demeanor didn't change at all, but inside he was quaking with rage. How dare Celine call him here when he had expressly instructed her not to? And how dare Andrea keep the messages from him?

Celine turned her face upward. "My poor darling, did you think I'd abandoned you?"

I really hadn't given you any thought at all. He briefly fantasized about saying it aloud. He enjoyed picturing her crestfallen face and punctured vanity. Instead, he bent his head over hers and cupped her chin with his hand. "I should have known you wouldn't abandon me," he breathed in a husky tone.

"It's that girl," Celine said petulantly. "She's trying to keep us apart. Can't you do something?"

"I'll do something," William promised, "when the time is right."

Her lips puckered, and she stood on her toes until their lips met. He returned the pressure and then broke away when the door suddenly opened.

Andrea stood in the doorway with a look of fury on her face. "Your time is up," she said through clenched teeth. Her eyes met William's with a malevolent and unwavering stare. Then they turned on Celine. "Hurry up. You've got to get out."

Celine reluctantly released her hold on William's arms and picked up her purse. "I'll talk to you later," she said. She lifted her nose and walked slowly out the door.

Andrea glared at William. "I'll take her out. You stay here until I come back for you."

William smiled. "I'll be waiting."

Chapter Six

"Danny Wyatt, please."

"Speaking." Danny put the submarine sandwich he was eating for dinner down and shifted the receiver of the phone so that it rested more comfortably between his shoulder and his ear.

"You don't know me, but my name is Tim. I'm on the football team."

"What can I do for you, Tim? And if this is the SVU Phone-a-Thon, I gave already."

There was a chuckle on the other end of the line. "Relax, man. I'm not looking for money. I'm just looking for a friend of Tom Watts's."

"That would be me." Danny took the receiver from its resting place and switched it to his other ear. "Is there some kind of a problem?"

"No," the guy said quickly. "Nothing like that. He's not there, is he?"

"No. He's at the library."

"Good. Because I wanted to talk to you privately about Tom."

"I don't usually discuss Tom without his knowledge," Danny said warily.

"Listen, I guess it's hard for a nonplayer to appreciate what Tom Watts means to this team," Tim continued. "But he's going to make a huge difference. To the team and to the school, too. Historically, in the years we've beaten State, alumni donations go up forty percent. That money gets spent in a lot of different departments, not just the athletic programs."

"All that sounds great," Danny said. "But what's this got to do with me?"

"Let me get to the point. If Tom's friends could rally for him at this game, they'd be doing a lot of good for him, and for the school, too."

"I still don't get what you're saying."

"Today, at practice, Tom mentioned how being back on the team is a big thrill and a dream come true. And he said the biggest thrill of all would be to see his friends cheering him on. But because of what happened to his family, he'd never ask."

Danny was starting to get the picture. "You're telling me Tom wants his friends to come see him play?"

"Sure. If you were the hero of the football team, wouldn't you want all your friends to see you play?"

Danny sat back in his chair and rocked slightly on the back legs. "I think you're right," Danny said slowly. "I had planned to drive to the game and just sort of watch unobtrusively from the back row, but maybe it would be better to make a big deal out of it. Get his friends together and let him know we're going to be there."

"How about making it a surprise?" Tim asked. "It would give him an incredible rush if he came running out of the locker room with the team and saw all of you sitting in the bleachers. Sort of a surprise party on wheels. Think you can arrange it?"

"Definitely," Danny answered. "And Tim, thanks for tipping me off. I wouldn't have thought of this on my own."

"That's what being teammates is about. Listen, I'll check back with you in a few days to see how everything's going."

"Wait a minute," Danny said into the phone. "Don't hang up."

"I'm here."

"What's your last name?" Danny asked.

"Hemphill," Tim replied.

"That's H-E-M-P-H-I-L-L," William said, his eyes darting toward the door when he heard the rattle of Andrea's key in the lock.

"I'll catch you later." He hung up the phone just as Andrea strode into the office.

She let out an infuriated snarl and lunged toward him.

William managed to sidestep Andrea in the nick of time. She missed her grasp and stumbled past him as he neatly rounded the desk, out of reach.

"Who do you think you are?" she panted. "How dare you use the phone in this office? How dare you use me and trick me?"

William drew himself up to his full height. "How dare you not give me my phone messages."

"You're not even supposed to be getting phone calls!" she bellowed.

William lifted his brow. "If I were you, I'd keep my voice down. I don't think either one of us is going to fare well if someone realizes you've been helping me."

Andrea's face paled, and she took several

deep breaths. "We're finished, William. *You're* finished."

"Andrea," he began, taking a tentative step forward. "Let's not argue. Celine is a source of valuable information. I had to . . ."

"Had to kiss her?" Andrea spat. "Bull. You're a big phony, William. I don't believe you're a political prisoner. I think you're a self-deluded nutcase like everybody else in this ward."

William felt the vein in his temple begin to throb. "Shut up."

Andrea ignored him.

"You're not a spy," she went on. "You're exactly what your file says you are. A lunatic."

"I am *not* a lunatic!" William seethed, bringing his fist down on the desk. "How dare you lump me together with the revolting collection of miscreants that people this hellhole?"

There was a strange smile on her face. "Yes, you are a lunatic," she taunted. "According to your file, you're a *paranoid schizophrenic with delusions of omnipotence.*"

William began moving toward her. "Stop using words you don't even understand."

"Oh, I understand everything. You don't have any power at all. Not without me. And you know what I say? I say you're never leaving this place again. Hear? Never."

His left eye had developed a tic, and blood was rushing toward his brain. "You don't know who you're dealing with," he raged.

"*You* don't know who *you're* dealing with, pal," she said, lifting her lip in a sneer. "But I know what I'm dealing with. I'm dealing with one more cuckoo who thinks he's Napoleon. You're insane and . . ."

William's hands were around her neck before she even had time to recoil. "Shut up!" he screamed. "Don't ever call me insane!"

Her eyes bulged with pain, and her fingers clawed at his hands. She made a panicky, gargling sound in the back of her throat. Her bulky body jerked away, pulling them both off balance.

They fell to the floor with a heavy crash, but William held on tight. He couldn't see her face anymore. All he could see was a misty, hazy veil of red. Her legs kicked and scissored, and they flipped over, with Andrea lying on top of him and pounding at his face. But William squeezed tighter and tighter. It was time to put an end to her witless, brainless, and joyless existence.

Her body gave one final lurch before she went limp.

William released his grasp and sat back, staring at her in fascination. She was dead. There was no doubt about it. Her eyes seemed to be looking at a point on the wall somewhere over William's head.

He leaned forward and closed her eyes with his fingertips. "Good night, Andrea," he said softly.

There was no time to waste now. He had to act fast. His hands searched Andrea's pockets, locating the things he was going to need. A wad of money and a heavy set of keys.

William stepped out of the office and closed the door behind him. Then he silently made his way down the hall toward the first of a series of locked doors. He fit the first key into the lock and opened the door easily. Around the corner was an employee lounge.

William opened the door and peered into the empty room. He hurried toward the bank of lockers provided for employees and deliberated. "Let's see, now. . . . Door number one? . . . Door number two? . . . Or door number three? . . . I think I'll take door number three." He opened the locker and smiled.

Inside the locker was a pair of jeans, a sweatshirt, and sneakers. He was feeling good now. Feeling like the old William White, who had ruled an entire campus and inspired fear in lesser mortals.

William slipped off his white cotton pajamas and changed into the street clothes. A fat wallet in the back pocket of the jeans held more money, a driver's license, credit cards, and an insurance card covering a blue GM truck.

Perfect.

William left the lounge and crossed the hall. The third key on Andrea's key ring fit the supply-closet door. He reached in and gathered several bottles of the potent barbiturate that was used to calm violent patients.

William felt like a rolling machine gathering momentum. He was moving faster and more efficiently as the seconds ticked by.

The last door was only yards away, and William forced himself to keep moving as if he had every right to walk through it. He couldn't afford to look nervous or tentative. But he had to hurry. There was an orderly making rounds in the ward, and it was only a matter of minutes—seconds, perhaps—before his disappearance was discovered and Andrea's body found.

The last security door was heavy steel with a bulletproof glass inset. Through the window, he could see Otto, a three-hundred-pound orderly, sitting at a desk. His head was bent over a magazine.

For the first time in this adventure, William felt a sense of trepidation. All hinged on his ability to get past Otto.

William put a key into the lock. He heard the tumblers click easily into place.

Otto's head lifted curiously. At the exact second that his eyes met William's, there was a loud cry from inside the ward. *"Escape!"*

Otto's brow wrinkled. "Hey, hold it," he warned, pulling his bulk up out of the chair just as somebody inside the ward hit the panic button, setting off an alarm loud enough to split the eardrums.

William lost no time. He lifted his elbow with a savage jerk and caught Otto under the jaw. He heard the loud click as Otto's lower teeth met his upper teeth and the ex-wrestler teetered backward.

William lunged forward, breaking into a run. Behind him, he heard footsteps. He took a quick look over his shoulder. Five orderlies were on his trail now.

Automatic doors in every hallway were sliding shut as the escape-prevention mechanisms moved into action. William turned a corner, lowered his head, and doubled his speed. At the end of the hall, a metal door was coming down like a garage door. "No!" he screamed.

There was a reverberating explosion as the door connected with the floor, sealing off the exit. William turned, his back against the security wall. His eyes darted back and forth, noting the glass walls on either side of the hallway.

William closed his eyes, mentally reconstructing the layout of the institution. If his guess was correct, he was now in the southwest corner of the estate.

He ran toward the window, covering his face with his hands. The glass broke upon impact with a splintering sound that seemed to echo on and on forever. There was a brief and euphoric falling sensation and then a series of painful pricks as he fell into the thick, two-story box-wood hedge.

He lay there for a moment, stunned. Voices coming through the broken window above him jolted him back into action. William struggled out of the hedge, blinking away the rivulets of blood that dripped from a hundred tiny cuts and scratches. He had no broken bones—and that meant he was still in business.

Floodlights swept the lawn as William darted from the shadow of one tree to another until he reached the perimeter of the parking lot. It took only two seconds to locate the blue truck and even less time to get it started.

The alarm bells sounded fainter and fainter as he hurtled out of the parking lot and down the road to the front gate. They would be waiting for him, he knew. But would they shoot?

He pushed his foot down on the gas pedal and increased his speed. There was only one way to find out.

As he approached the gate, he turned the truck lights on. As he had expected, there were three security guards standing in the road with their guns leveled at him.

His foot came down heavily on the gas pedal. The truck actually left the ground as it lurched forward and sent the guards scattering in every direction.

The pickup flew through the wrought-iron front gate, breaking it open as sirens filled the night air. William rolled down his window. The noise was coming from the direction of town. The institution had called for police help, which meant the main road was no longer an option.

William yanked the wheel and turned onto a

dirt road that led to a rickety bridge. A bridge that spanned a deep gorge and led into a thickly wooded state park on the other side. If he could make it into the woods without being followed, he could abandon the truck and continue on foot.

Too late, he realized he should have killed his lights. A security vehicle was on his trail.

The truck barreled along the dirt road, and William bounced around in the cab, his head thumping the roof. The oscillating scream of sirens behind him became louder, and William watched in the rearview mirror as a caravan of flashing lights joined the chase.

The bridge came into sight, and William made a quick decision. He steered with his right hand and gripped the handle of the door with his left.

As soon as he passed beneath the thick leafy overhang that created a shadowy gateway to the bridge, he jerked the handle and dove sideways out the door.

The rear wheels missed him by inches, and William rolled out of the road just as beams from a pursuing vehicle lit the area.

He rolled into a ditch and watched as the blue truck continued toward the bridge at top speed, missed the entrance, and dove over the side of the gorge. He heard it crash into the boulders below. There was a brief moment of silence before the gas tank exploded, sending a geyser of twisted metal and fire toward the sky.

William ran, doubling back toward the institution. They wouldn't be looking for him there. Or anywhere else for that matter.

Because William White was now officially dead.

Chapter Seven

"You should feel good."

"Good? That somebody's dead?"

"All right, *good*'s probably not the right word. '*Relieved,*' maybe?"

Elizabeth nodded reluctantly and stared at the newspaper that featured a front-page account of William's escape and suicide. Jessica had found it when she opened the door. Someone had left it outside their room early this morning. "You're right. But that makes me feel like a horrible person."

"The guy tried to kill you," Jessica pointed out. "He was a homicidal maniac. Feeling relieved that he's gone doesn't make you a horrible person. It makes you a human."

Elizabeth smiled. "Thanks, Jess. I guess I'm just so blown away by this I don't know what I'm feeling."

There was a knock on the door—for about the fifteenth time that morning. Elizabeth rolled her eyes. William's attempt to murder Elizabeth had been front-page news a while back. Now everybody was stopping by to see if she'd heard what happened.

Jessica walked over to the door. "We know," she said as she opened it. "Oh, it's you."

Elizabeth looked up as Tom stepped into the room, his face full of concern. "Are you OK?"

"I'm OK, but I'm in major shock."

Tom walked over and held out his arms. Elizabeth stepped inside his embrace and wound her arms around his waist. "I never thought I'd say I was glad somebody died, but I'm glad William White is dead. There was always this nagging fear that he would manage to escape. And he did. But thank goodness he didn't get far."

"I know, Liz. I feel the same way." Tom ran his hands up and down her back, unknotting her tense muscles.

Elizabeth felt as if she'd just let go of a huge and heavy burden. She sagged slightly, and Tom helped her to a chair.

Jessica hovered at his elbow. "Hey, Lizzie, are you OK? Say something."

"I'm OK. I'm just . . . just . . ."

"Hungry, probably," Tom said briskly. He pulled on her arm and she stood. "Let's go get some breakfast. You'll feel better after you eat."

"I'm not sure I'm up to going to the cafeteria," Elizabeth protested. "People are going to be bombarding me with questions."

"I'll protect you," Tom reassured her. "And if you go into hiding, it'll just make people more curious about you. What you want is for this to blow over as soon as possible."

Elizabeth still felt hesitant.

"I know what it's like to be the object of morbid curiosity," he said softly. "Believe me, if you fight it, you lose. It's better to be seen going on with your life."

"He's right," Jessica said. "We'll all go. Safety in numbers."

An hour and a half later, Elizabeth sat in the empty bleachers of the stadium watching Tom practice with the team. In spite of her certainty that William White was dead, she was reluctant to let Tom get too far away.

He'd been right about breakfast. She'd felt better after eating a few pancakes and drinking some coffee. And the few people who had commented to her about William had been so full of genuine concern for her that it had been impossible to take offense.

A volley of shouts from the field diverted her attention, and several squatting players burst into action. As she watched, Tom caught a pass and began running for the goal line. Two linebackers tried to stop him, but Tom was too fast and too strong. He plowed forward, dragging the linebackers from the tail of his jersey.

"He's really good, isn't he?"

Elizabeth jumped and let out a shriek.

"Hey, hey! It's me. Relax."

Elizabeth took a couple of panting breaths while her heartbeat returned to normal.

"I'm sorry," Danny said. "I thought you saw me coming up the stands."

Elizabeth shook her head. "No. I guess I was lost in my own thoughts and . . ." She forced a laugh. "You must think I'm nuts."

"Nope. I think you've been on your guard for so long, it's hard to suddenly turn it off."

Elizabeth nodded.

"Well, I think I've got an idea that will take your mind off William White. A surefire, guaranteed-to-bring-a-smile-to-your-face proposal."

"Sounds good," Elizabeth agreed. "Make the pitch."

"You, me, Isabella, Jessica, Maia, Denise,

Winston, Nina, Bryan, and a minivan."

"A road trip?"

"A road trip. To watch our mutual friend, Tom Watts, make his debut in the all-important SVU-versus-State competition."

"This is OK with Tom?"

"Apparently so—according to Tim Hemphill."

"Who's that?"

"A teammate of Tom's." Danny craned his neck, watching the players. "He called me and said that Tom really wants his friends there at the game."

"That doesn't seem like Tom," she said slowly.

"No. But after the events of the last few days, I'm ready to admit I'm not an expert on what Tom's thinking and feeling."

"That makes two of us," Elizabeth muttered.

"Do I hear a note of resentment?"

"No. Frustration."

"So will you help me put together a surprise package on wheels?"

Elizabeth smiled. It *would* be fun to surprise Tom on his big day. And it would take her mind off William White and Todd Wilkins.

". . . annnnndddd flip *again*," Denise urged.

Winston curled his body, put every ounce of

bounce into it, and just missed executing a third back flip. "Yeoww!" he cried as he tumbled onto the turf and lay there in a heap.

Denise came rushing over and fell to her knees beside him. "Winnie? Are you all right?"

"Sure, I'm all right. For a pretzel." Winston managed to extricate his legs from his arms and stretched to get the kinks out.

They were on the soccer field behind the athletic complex, practicing for the Braino tryouts, along with several other Braino hopefuls.

Winston wished he'd never started this Braino business. He'd thought it would be fun and a good way to impress Denise. But so far, it had been a lot of hard hours of physical exertion. And as far as impressing Denise went, he was so outclassed by the competition, it was laughable.

Winston watched the others with a gloomy eye. There was a blond surfer dude with a Gumby body. Tall, with long arms and long legs that could do amazing things.

Then there was the girl. An Amazonian gymnast. Six feet tall, and man, could she do a back flip. "Affirmative action's probably got me blown out of the water already," he grumbled.

"What does that mean?"

"As far as I know, there's never been a female

Braino—which probably means they're going to give it to a girl."

"Oh, quit complaining and practice," Denise ordered.

"It's a waste of time," Winston argued. "Look around, Denise. Some of these people are incredible."

"I think *you're* pretty incredible," she said with a sweet smile on her face.

"Really?"

"Really." Her smile disappeared and turned into a fierce scowl. "Now, get back to work."

"Denise! I've been flipping and cartwheeling all morning. I'm motion-sick."

"Winston," she pleaded. "You have no idea how good you are. Don't give up now. *Please!*"

"What have I got that none of these other people have got?" he demanded.

"You mean besides me?"

Winston smiled. It drove him crazy when Denise said things like that. He never knew how serious she was. Did he have her? Did he really? "Can we be serious for a minute? They've got better moves. They're more talented gymnasts. They're stronger."

"OK," Denise agreed. "So some of them have bigger muscles and better gymnastic backgrounds. But they don't have your . . . your . . . your . . ."

Denise squinched her face and waved her hands, as if searching for just the right word.

"My what?"

"Your *personality*."

Winston rolled his eyes. *Geez. How incredibly anticlimactic.* "That's *it*? They don't have my *personality*? You really know how to make a guy feel good."

Denise giggled. "Charisma's not all that easy to come by, Win."

"Charisma! That's better." He repeated the word, giving the *r* a good roll. "Cha*rrrr*isma! It sounds very . . . *macho*!" He pounded his chest, then executed a perfect back flip.

Light laughter floated in his direction. Elizabeth Wakefield was walking toward them, smiling and applauding.

"All right!" Elizabeth crowed. "I didn't know you were trying out for Braino."

"Think he's got a shot?" Denise asked.

"I think he'd be the best Braino in history." Elizabeth gave Denise a friendly smile. "I guess you know Winston was the class clown in high school?"

Winston put his arm around Denise and began to feel a little better. Being admired by two girls who were so pretty almost made it worth the humiliating defeat he was going to endure tomorrow. "She knows," he answered. "But she loves me anyway." His voice broke slightly on the word *loves*, but neither girl seemed to notice.

Denise's sharp elbow poked him in the ribs. "Winston, are you listening?"

"No. Sorry. What did I miss?"

"We're going to the State game," she said. "With a bunch of Tom's friends."

"That sounds like fun," Winston said happily. "Can we go now?"

"What? And miss the Braino tryouts?" Elizabeth teased. "Danny's taking care of most of the arrangements," she said in a more serious tone. "He'll give you a call. In the meantime, don't talk about it, because we want it to be a surprise."

Winston elaborately pretended to lock his lips and throw away the key. "Two weeks of mime school," he whispered to Denise.

The girls laughed and Elizabeth lifted her hand. "OK, then. I'm off." She patted Winston on the shoulder. "Good luck tomorrow."

As Elizabeth walked away, Denise put her hands on her hips. "Break time is over, Egbert. Let's see another flip."

Winston sighed. By this time tomorrow, he'd be lucky if he could walk, much less do a back flip.

*   *   *

Elizabeth stopped in her tracks and turned around, her eyes searching the crowded walkway. Students flowed in every direction across the busy quad. Had one of them been following her?

Since leaving the soccer field, she'd sensed that someone was behind her. Was she paranoid? Or was this some kind of logical emotional aftermath to William White's death?

She turned back in the direction of her dorm. She had to cross a long stretch of wooded park to get to Dickenson Hall.

Something instinctive told her to run. She didn't even look backward. She just took off across the park. She could hear feet pounding the ground behind her. Someone *had* been following her. Elizabeth dropped her books and let out a shriek. "Leave me alone!" A hand caught the back of her sweater and she twisted violently, pulling her arms from the sweater and lifting her fists to fight off the attacker.

Her long blond hair wrapped around her eyes, blinding her. Someone grabbed her hands and held them tight as she struggled. "Elizabeth!" he shouted. "Elizabeth, stop it. It's me. It's me, Todd."

She felt his grasp loosen, and she jerked away,

clawing her hair away from her face. Todd stepped back, his face alarmed. "Elizabeth, calm down. I'm sorry I scared you."

"Why were you following me?" she shouted. "What do you want?"

"Just to . . . to . . . say hello. To talk," Todd stuttered.

"Hello," Elizabeth said in a choking voice. She snatched her backpack and sweater off the ground. "And good-bye. I've had enough for one day, so leave me alone. OK?" Elizabeth broke into a run, tears streaming down her face. She was being followed, not just by Todd but by the ghost of William White.

Elizabeth slowed and wiped her eyes when she saw Jessica at the entrance to their dorm.

"You look terrible," Jessica commented. "You need to relax, Liz."

"I'm trying. But I'm so nervous I feel like I'm about to jump out of my skin. And it doesn't help to have Todd skulking around the bushes behind me."

"Todd!"

Elizabeth nodded. "He was following me."

"Elizabeth, you should tell Tom."

"No," Elizabeth said in a firm voice. She wasn't exactly sure why she felt as strongly as she did about it, but she didn't want to discuss

Todd with Tom. No matter how low Todd had sunk, she hated to make him look worse than he already did.

The girls stepped into the elevator, and Jessica pushed the button. Jessica said nothing as they rode to their floor, but Elizabeth could sense her disapproval.

When they reached their room, Jessica walked through the door first and let out a little outraged shriek. "I can't believe this!"

Elizabeth's eyes immediately found the object of Jessica's disgust. A Ken doll in a football uniform lay on Elizabeth's bed. The head had been twisted off and lay beside the decapitated body.

"Is this supposed to be some kind of threat against Tom?" Jessica asked.

Elizabeth threw her books to floor. "This does it. I've cut Todd Wilkins enough slack. It's take-the-consequences time." She marched over to the phone and punched in three numbers.

On the second ring, a deep voice answered. "Hello. Security."

Chapter Eight

"William?" The cart creaked slightly as Celine worked her way up and down the aisles of bookshelves. "William?" she whispered again.

He couldn't be dead. Not William White.

Oh, sure. That's what the paper had said. But like Granny Boudreaux always said, you can't believe everything you read.

William was immortal. He was indestructible. He was alive, and Celine knew it. *Granny Boudreaux always said that love is a terrible thing. And now I know why. It's terrible to need someone as much as you need food and water.*

But Celine did love William. And she did need him. She needed his plots. His plans. His grand schemes. "I don't know how you did it, sweetie," she whispered through thickly painted lips, "but you fooled 'em. Fooled everybody but little ole Celine. Come out, William. Come out and see me, sweetheart."

She wondered if he was watching her, and she hitched up her skirt for effect. He'd be pretty shaken up by all the commotion. And maybe a little reluctant to trust her.

Mr. White apparently escaped the institution in which he had been confined after brutally murdering the orderly on duty, the newspaper had said.

Had he murdered that girl—Andrea?

She pushed the thought to the back of her mind. Andrea was a blot on the landscape, a meddler and a nuisance. But she hated to think that William had murdered her on Celine's account. Live and let live—that had always been Celine's motto.

She stopped at the shelf for oversized books and restored some large art books to their proper place. The sound of something clattering to the floor caught her attention, and she pushed her cart in the direction of the sound.

Celine's perfectly chiseled, upturned nose quivered. He had been here. Been here within the last few seconds. "William?" she called out in a louder voice, pushing her cart through a door. The room was dark, and filled with rows of shelves that reached to the ceiling. "William,

116

honey, don't make me chase you."

She heard the creaking noise of a door and then a slam.

Celine hurried toward the old manuscript and map room and looked around. Then she pushed the cart toward the door that led to the maintenance area, with her heart hammering in her chest. Was he trying to elude her? Or was he beckoning her to follow?

Tentatively, she opened the door and stepped inside the dim hallway. Someone had repaired the light since she had last been in here. "William?" The door slowly swung shut behind her and closed with a reverberating bang. The dull roar of machinery hummed in a syncopated rhythm, and Celine felt her body begin to pulsate in response. Her breath was shallow, and she began to tremble with fear and anticipation. "William," she said, struggling to keep her voice steady, "I know you're in here."

A long shadow fell across the floor, and Celine held her breath as William stepped out from behind a generator. "Where is your cart?" he asked without preamble.

"I left it outside the door," she answered breathlessly.

"What a foolish thing to do. Bring it in here. Someone might see it and get curious."

Celine whirled around on her stiletto heels, opened the door, and peered out into the library. There was no one in the map room. She reached out and pulled the cart into the hallway. "There's no one out there," she whispered. "You're safe."

"Did you tell anyone that I was here? That I was alive?"

His expression was so tense and forbidding that Celine felt the hairs on the back of her neck rise. "No. Of course not."

William's face relaxed. "Good."

Celine noticed that his arm was held behind his back. "Are you hurt?" she asked.

He shook his head. "No. Just prepared to celebrate." He brought his hand out and held up a bottle of champagne and two glasses. "Champagne?"

Celine laughed appreciatively as William handed her a glass and poured the bubbling liquid until it foamed. He filled his own glass, then clinked it against hers. "Here's to the late, great William White. May he rest in peace."

"What now?" she asked, leaning back against the wall.

William sat on the edge of the library cart, crossed his legs, and sipped thoughtfully. "I've got a few things to finish up here, then I thought I'd leave the country."

"Alone?" she asked, with a teasing smile on her face.

He shook his head. "No. Not alone. I'll be taking someone with me. Someone extremely special."

Celine lifted her glass and gave him a big-eyed look as she took a sip. She didn't mind leaving Sweet Valley University one bit. College wasn't her cup of tea. She'd had it with the teachers, the snotty sorority types, and especially the boring intellectual snobs like Elizabeth Wakefield.

Still, it was never a good idea to let a man take you for granted. "What if she doesn't want to go?" she asked coyly.

William's face never changed expression. "I'll kill her," he said simply.

Celine's heart gave a terrified thump. She dropped her glass, and it shattered into a million pieces. "You wouldn't really?"

He held up his full glass and examined it in the dim light. "Yes. Of course, I'd kill myself, too. Elizabeth and I will either live together—or die together. The choice will be hers."

"Elizabeth!" Celine cried. She felt as if she'd been punched in the stomach. The hallway seemed to shift slightly, and she put her hand against the wall to steady herself. "I thought you hated her," she choked.

William gave her a bland smile. "Why would you think that?"

"The dolls. The tricks. The . . ."

William shrugged. "Just my way of staying in touch." His face darkened slightly. "My way of letting her know that I'm serious."

The roof was spinning now. Celine felt so dizzy, she was almost ill. "I thought you loved me!" she wailed. "I thought you needed me. . . ."

William reached out and tilted her chin up with one finger. "Oh, I do need you, Celine. I need you very much."

Celine felt her knees buckle, and her eyelids began to droop. She realized it wasn't just the shock of hearing that William was in love with Elizabeth that was making her feel so strange. It was something else. Something physical. *The champagne,* her mind shrieked. *There was something in the champagne.*

"It looks like you're going, Celine," William said pleasantly. "I'm sorry I had to kill you, but I've tried to make it as painless as possible."

The light began to disappear, shrinking until she could only see a tiny pinhole of light. She couldn't move or speak, but nonetheless she felt light as a feather and began to float upward and away from the scene. From somewhere high in the air, she watched William lift her limp body, drop it into the library cart, and begin wheeling it away.

"We could use some more glasses out here," Joe said, swiping at the counter with a discolored bar rag.

"I'll take care of it right away," Todd agreed. He wrung out the mop he'd been using and walked through the swinging door that led to the kitchen.

The dishwasher still had a couple of minutes to run, so Todd looked around the kitchen to see if there was some two-minute chore he could perform.

There wasn't.

There were plenty of two-*hour* chores—but no two-*minute* chores. The kitchen was as filthy and cluttered as everything else in Joe's Pub.

From the way Joe had described the place over the phone, Todd had expected an upscale sports bar and grill full of college kids and yuppies.

But what he had found was a small, run-down hole-in-the-wall run by a large, gruff—but apparently well-meaning—guy named Joe.

He'd given Todd a warm greeting when he arrived and shown him up to the room over the bar with great ceremony. Todd had managed to smile and sound grateful, but his heart had sunk when he saw the small windowless closet where he'd be sleeping.

The furnishings consisted of a lumpy bare mattress on a rusty single bed frame. There was no desk, or dresser, or even a chair. The atmosphere was so depressing that Todd hadn't managed to sleep a wink.

He leaned back against the sink and crossed his arms over his chest, thinking. He was absolutely exhausted, but his mind kept going around and around in circles. He'd asked around the street, but nobody had heard of Henry, the guy he had had coffee with.

For about the five hundredth time, he wondered who had it in for him enough to do something like that. And how was he going to prove he hadn't stolen the car?

He examined his reflection in the cracked mirror that hung over the kitchen sink. No wonder Elizabeth had run away from him today. He looked demented. There were dark circles under his eyes, and unattractive stubble on his cheeks, and his color was terrible. No wonder.

The dishwasher clicked off, and Todd began transferring glasses from the dishwasher to a tray. He'd always thought working in a bar was kind of glamorous. Now he knew better. One more career option he could cross off his list.

Actually, that list was getting shorter and shorter. If he actually wound up convicted of car theft, it would be a felony. And a felony conviction would effectively exclude him from a lot of careers, law and banking among them.

He balanced the tray on his shoulder and headed toward the swinging door. He'd learned from experience—two head-on collisions with Joe—that it was best to look through the round glass window to make sure no one was coming in while he was going out.

Todd peered through the glass, and his eyes widened. Joe was talking to somebody at the door. Somebody who looked very familiar. As he watched, a man wearing sunglasses and a baseball cap handed a thick wad of money to Joe.

Todd raced through the door, dropping the tray. The guy in the baseball hat took one look, then broke into a run. Todd would have caught him if Joe hadn't inserted his large body between Todd and the door.

"Get out of the way!" Todd yelled.

"Hold it," Joe cautioned, grabbing Todd by the back of his collar.

"That guy set me up. Let me go!"

But Joe held on tight and gave Todd a savage

shake. "Calm down," he ordered, letting go of Todd so suddenly that he fell to the floor, raising a cloud of grimy bar dust.

"Who is that guy?" Todd demanded through gritted teeth.

"Your only friend," Joe said.

"Friend? What are you talking about?"

"He felt bad about what happened with the car."

"He set me up with that car."

"It was an accident. He says somebody loaned him the car. He didn't know it was stolen either."

"That's bull."

"Look, all I know is that he felt bad about you getting expelled, and he's trying to make it up to you."

"What was that money?"

"Your rent."

"Rent? I thought you were lending me the room."

"He set it up. He asked me to call you and offer you a job and a room, OK? He said he'd cover all the expenses."

"Who is he?"

Joe shrugged. "In this bar it's not healthy to ask a lot of questions—you know what I mean?" He leaned over and grabbed Todd's arm to help him to his feet.

"Because of that *friend*, I might wind up with a felony conviction," Todd seethed.

Joe put a hand on his shoulder. "Go upstairs. Get some rest."

Todd nodded. He would go upstairs. Force himself to sleep. Then he'd get out and prowl every bar, restaurant, club, alley, and side street until he found that guy.

His feet felt like concrete blocks as he climbed the outside steps to the room. It was dark in his room, and when he stepped inside, he stumbled against something on the floor.

His hand fumbled at the wall until he flicked the overhead light on. "Oh, no!" He fell back, gasping. Celine Boudreaux lay on the floor of his room like a rag doll. "No," he whispered hoarsely, kneeling down beside her. "It can't be." He lifted a limp wrist and felt for a pulse. Nothing. He put his fingertips to the side of her neck. Still no pulse.

She was dead. Her arms and legs were cold, and her face looked as if it were made of wax.

Todd's mind began spinning. What had happened to Celine? And how had she gotten here?

There was a loud knock at the door. Todd's heart began to race. What should he do?

There was a second knock. "Mr. Wilkins. Mr. Wilkins, are you in there?"

Slowly, Todd rose to his feet, went to the door, and opened it a crack. Two uniformed policemen stood on the landing. "Todd Wilkins?"

His voice trembled when he spoke. "Yes?"

One of the police officers shifted his stance slightly and rested his hands on his hips. "We've been asked by Sweet Valley University Security to locate you."

"Why?"

"Are you aware that stalking someone is now a crime?" the second officer asked.

"I haven't been stalking anybody." His eyes darted from one officer's face to the other. "Really!" he added lamely.

"Do you mind if we come inside and look around?" the first officer asked.

"Ummmm."

"Is there something in your room that you'd rather us not see?"

Todd began to close the door, but one of them moved quickly forward and stuck his foot in the door. "We'd like to take a look around."

Todd let out a yell and rushed them. Both officers tumbled backward. Todd leapt over their fallen bodies at the foot of the stairs and took off at a run.

"Freeze!" he heard them yell behind him.

But Todd didn't stop. As soon as he hit the

street, he headed directly toward a group of girls who were walking up the sidewalk. He felt sure the police wouldn't shoot into a crowd.

The girls screamed as he broke through them and pounded around the corner. Somehow he had to elude the police long enough to find the guy in the baseball hat.

First the car. Now a body.

What was this guy trying to do to him?

And why? *Why?*

Chapter Nine

"So can I count on you guys to come?"

Noah put down his napkin and looked at Alexandra. "I think it sounds like fun."

"It sounds great," Alexandra agreed. "And I'd like to see the State campus. It's supposed to be really beautiful."

Isabella gave Alexandra's hand a squeeze. "I'm glad you're coming," she said in a low voice, as Danny and Noah launched into a long discussion about time, places, and provisions.

It was still fairly early, and most of the tables in the cafeteria were empty. The heavy traffic wouldn't start for another half hour.

She and Noah had met for an early breakfast. Soon after they'd arrived, Danny and Isabella had come over and joined them at their table.

Both Alexandra and Isabella were Thetas.

But Isabella was older and far more glamorous than Alexandra could ever hope to be. It was extremely flattering to Alexandra that Isabella had been seeking out her company recently. And she was even more flattered that Isabella and Danny were inviting her and Noah along on the road trip. "Thanks for including us," Alexandra said to Isabella.

"It'll be fun. Four Thetas. You, Jessica, me, and Denise."

Alexandra took a sip of her coffee. "You and Denise have been really great over the last few weeks. Thanks for not giving up on me. I know I was shaping up to be a total washout as a pledge."

"Washouts don't stand up to Alison the way you did," Isabella said, referring to Alexandra's courageous defense of Jessica in front of the Theta vice president, Alison Quinn. "If it hadn't been for you, Jessica would have been voted out of the Thetas. Then Alison and her snobby friends would have been bullying the whole sorority by now. You helped us all."

"And you really helped me," Alexandra answered. "What you said about my drinking helped me get focused on getting my life straightened out."

Isabella nodded toward Noah, who was still

engrossed in animated conversation with Danny. "Looks like things are straightening out very well."

Alexandra felt a flush creep up the back of her neck. "It's all pretty new," she confided. "We're still getting to know each other."

"Sometimes a group outing helps a couple bond," Isabella commented. "I know that was true for me and Danny."

Before Alexandra could respond, Danny had spotted Maia Stillwater and waved her over. Behind her came Bryan Nelson and Nina Harper. Nina was Elizabeth's best friend, and Bryan was her boyfriend, as well as the president of the Black Students Union.

"Greetings," Danny said with a big smile. "Sit down and get ready to sign up."

"Uh-oh," Bryan groaned. "Is it Rally Day already? OK. OK. Put me down for the potato-sack race. But I am not—I repeat, *not*—going to roll an egg across the quad with my nose."

Everybody laughed as Noah and Isabella pulled a second table over so that there would be room for everybody. Nina gave Alexandra a broad smile and a friendly greeting as she removed her plate of oatmeal, grapefruit, and coffee from her tray.

"It's not Rally Day," Danny explained. "But

I am begging everyone to rally. I'm organizing a group to go to the game and be Tom Watts's personal cheering section."

"All right!" Nina nodded happily, taking a seat between Maia and Bryan. "Good plan. I'm in."

"Me too," Bryan added immediately. "Where she goes, I go—if I'm lucky."

"Maia?" Danny prompted.

She shook her head. "No, thanks. I'm not too hot on the football team right now."

There was an awkward silence. Maia's stunning testimony at James Montgomery's hearing had shaken the campus to its foundation. Jessica's accusation of sexual assault had been dismissed until Maia had come forward and tearfully revealed that James had raped her several weeks before.

The silence was broken by the jingle of Isabella's two gold bangles as she leaned over the table and put her hand over Maia's. "James Montgomery was one guy. Not the whole football team. This is for Tom. He's been through a rough time. He doesn't have a family anymore. But he does have friends—and his friends need to show him that they care."

"And it'll be *fun*," Nina added in a cheerful voice. "We'll all sit together and form our own cheering section."

"Please come," Alexandra said softly. "We'll all have a better time if you do. We haven't seen much of you in the last few weeks."

"And believe me, nobody will bother you," Bryan promised. "You'll have a squad of the best bodyguards on campus. Right, Danny?"

"Right," Danny agreed with a reassuring wink.

Maia lifted her face and smiled. "OK. You talked me into it."

Everybody applauded and burst into excited chatter. Alexandra looked over and caught Noah staring at her with his fork dangling between his plate and his mouth. A smile played around the corners of her lips. If she wasn't mistaken, that was the look of a man who was in love—and he was in love with her.

"Got room for us?" a familiar voice asked.

"You bet," Noah said, immediately taking his plate and sliding sideways.

Everybody laughed and pretended to complain as they shifted and squeezed together to make room for Denise and Winston.

"We must look pretty ridiculous." Noah chuckled.

"How big, exactly, is the minivan?" Isabella asked Danny in a wry voice.

"Well, you can count Winston out," Denise said.

"Oh, no!" everybody cried.

"You're not dropping out on us, are you?" Isabella wailed.

Denise smiled. "No, but he'll be driving the Brainmobile."

Winston put his head into his hands. "That's it. You've jinxed it."

Everybody cracked up, and Nina rolled her eyes. "No, she hasn't. When are the tryouts?"

"In about an hour," Winston whimpered.

"Hey, there's Jessica," Danny said, interrupting.

Alexandra looked over and saw Jessica hurrying across the cafeteria with a newspaper in her hand and a frown on her face. "Jessica! Over here."

Jessica's face turned toward the group and she hurried toward them.

"Sit," Isabella invited.

"I can't. I need to find Elizabeth."

"Why? What's the matter?" Alexandra asked, noticing the white, tense look on Jessica's face.

Jessica held up the newspaper so that the group could see the picture of Todd Wilkins that was splashed across the front page. "There's a warrant out for his arrest."

"What for?"

"For the attempted murder of Celine Boudreaux," she answered grimly.

"Attempted murder," said the paper.

Attempted?

William crushed the newspaper into a ball and ground his teeth in anger. When William White attempted something, he was used to succeeding. Celine was supposed to be dead.

That's what one got for trying to be a nice guy, he thought angrily. If he had had any sense, he would have strangled her, too.

All his planning and plotting had gone like clockwork—until now.

How could he have been so clumsy? So careless?

Ah, well, hindsight was twenty-twenty. Things like this were going to happen from time to time. He'd just have to do his best to remedy the situation.

A pay phone stood at the corner, and William hurried toward it, fishing a quarter from the depths of his pocket.

"Patient Information," announced a pleasant female voice.

"Could you please connect me with Celine Boudreaux's room?"

"That's room three twenty-four," the woman said. "One moment."

There was a series of electronic beeps, and

then a man answered. "Nurses' Station. May I help you?"

"I was calling Celine Boudreaux."

"Ms. Boudreaux's calls are being routed through here. Who's calling, please?"

"This is Willy Bob Boudreaux, Celine's brother." William spoke in a drawling and worried voice. "I'm in Memphis right now waiting for a plane to Sweet Valley. Can you tell me anything about my sister's condition?"

"Let me connect you with her doctor," the voice suggested.

William tapped his foot and listened impatiently as the Mantovani orchestra sawed its way through a medley of early Beatles songs. Finally, the phone gave an electronic bleep, and a brisk female voice answered. "This is Dr. Ames. I understand you're a member of Celine Boudreaux's family?"

"Yes. I'm her brother. What in the world happened?" he gasped in a horrified voice.

"The police theorize that your sister was poisoned by a schoolmate," the doctor answered. "But I'm not prepared to comment on anything but her medical condition."

"Is she conscious? Has she spoken with the police?"

"No, Mr. Boudreaux. Your sister is in a coma and on life support."

"Is she expected to live?" William asked in a trembling voice.

There was a long pause at the other end of the line. "It's hard to predict in these cases," the doctor said in a softer, kinder tone. "Your sister is young, and her body is strong, but I would advise you to get here as soon as possible."

"Oh, I will," William answered, a grim smile spreading slowly across his face. "I'll be there just as soon as I can."

"Elizabeth. Cut it out. It's not your fault," Jessica insisted.

Elizabeth wiped her tears with a tissue. "It is too my fault," she said in a choking voice. "If I'd stopped to talk to Todd . . . if I'd listened to him instead of running away, then maybe . . . maybe . . ."

"Maybe he would have tried to kill you instead of Celine," Jessica finished in a brisk, matter-of-fact voice.

Elizabeth dropped her head in her hands and sobbed. "Todd would never hurt me."

"Are you kidding? Look at what he's put you through over the last few weeks. Those dolls. The notes. Those were threats, Elizabeth." Jessica threw up her hands in frustration. Why couldn't Elizabeth see that Todd Wilkins had been an accident waiting to happen?

"He needed help. I was supposed to be his friend. But instead of trying to help, I sicced Security on him. That level of rejection probably unhinged him. And now Celine might die because of me."

"Celine's body was already on the floor when the police got there," Jessica reminded her. "If you hadn't called Security, and the police hadn't gotten there when they did, Celine might be dead by now."

Elizabeth lifted her head and nodded. "That's true," she said hoarsely.

Encouraged, Jessica grabbed the box of Kleenex off the desk and handed it to Elizabeth. "Todd's been drinking heavily for a while now. We both know what alcohol can do to people," she added in a soft voice. She still hated talking about the drunken sexual assault that James Montgomery had attempted.

"I can't help feeling it's all connected," Elizabeth said slowly, walking to the window. "William killing that orderly and then himself. Todd trying to kill Celine." There was a long pause. "I guess we should just be glad Todd didn't kill himself, too." She turned to face Jessica. "Where do you think he is?"

"Probably on his way to Mexico," Jessica said, standing up and crossing her arms over her chest. "And there goes the bond you posted."

"The money doesn't matter," Elizabeth said wearily.

"It will to Mom and Dad when you have to ask them for next quarter's tuition again."

"I thought you were supposed to be making me feel better," Elizabeth complained.

There was a knock at the door, and they froze. Surely Todd wouldn't have the nerve to walk right up to Elizabeth's door and knock—would he?

Alarm and confusion were clearly at war with common sense in Elizabeth's breast. "It can't be him," she whispered. "Can it?"

"At this point, nothing would surprise me," Jessica said dryly. She put her finger to her lips, cautioning Elizabeth to be quiet, then she moved silently to the desk. She picked up the phone and dialed the first two numbers of the security office. "Who is it?" she called out, her finger hovering over the last digit.

"It's Alexandra," a quiet voice answered. "May I come in?"

Elizabeth's shoulders relaxed, and Jessica replaced the receiver with a sigh of relief.

Alexandra lifted her brows when the door

139

opened and gave Jessica an inquisitive look.

"She's upset but coping pretty well," Jessica muttered out of the side of her mouth, closing the door behind Alexandra.

"I heard that," Elizabeth said.

"I'd say that pretty much describes all of us," Alexandra said, stepping into the room. "I just came by to see if you'd heard anything new. And to say I'm sorry."

"We haven't heard anything new," Elizabeth said. "All we know is what we read in the paper. And I'm the one who's sorry—sorry about your tuition money. I feel like you never would have had to put up half the money if I hadn't."

"You're right. I would have put up all the money. So don't worry about it, OK?" She gave Elizabeth a warm smile. "In spite of everything, I still saw Todd as a hero. In a million years, I never would have seen this coming."

"Well, if we'd been using our heads we would have," Jessica said.

"What do you mean?"

Very quickly, Jessica explained to her about the dolls, the notes, the stalking.

Alexandra's mouth fell open. "Elizabeth! I had no idea it was that bad."

There was another knock on the door.

"I'll man the phone," Jessica said.

"I'll see who it is," Elizabeth volunteered.

Jessica punched in the Security number, and Elizabeth opened the door a tiny crack. Then it flew open, and Tom Watts was suddenly standing in the middle of the room, holding her sister in a tight embrace.

"I'm so sorry," Tom said, finally loosening his grip on Elizabeth.

Elizabeth's eyes were puffy from crying, but she still managed to convey a sense of self-possession. "I'm OK," she said.

"I don't think you are," Alexandra said. "I think you should talk to the police about getting some protection."

Jessica smacked her forehead. "Why didn't I think of that?"

"Hold it! Hold it!" Tom said. "Why does Elizabeth need police protection?"

"From Todd."

"What's Todd got to do with Elizabeth?"

Jessica saw her sister's eyes pleading with her not to tell. "I've got to tell him, Liz. He needs to know."

"Tell me what?" Tom demanded.

"Todd's been stalking Elizabeth."

"Stalking her?"

"Tell him." Jessica went to her closet and retrieved the decapitated Ken doll. "Look at this."

141

Tom recoiled. "What is that?"

"You," Jessica said simply.

"Jessica, please don't be melodramatic," Elizabeth begged.

"Your old boyfriend stalks you for weeks. He leaves all kinds of implied death threats. Then he tries to murder someone. I'd say that's pretty dramatic."

For a second, Tom looked as though he'd been hit over the head with a baseball bat. Slowly, he turned to Elizabeth. "How could you not tell me something like that?"

"Please don't get upset," Elizabeth pleaded.

"Yeah, please don't," Jessica echoed. "We're out of Kleenex."

A snort of laughter came from Alexandra's direction, and Jessica and Alexandra exchanged an amused look.

Tom's face broke into a reluctant smile. "All right. I won't go ballistic. But I think you should call the police and arrange for them to tail you."

"No," Elizabeth said emphatically.

"Why not?"

"Starting in two hours I've got back-to-back classes all day. That means I'll be surrounded by people."

Tom looked at his watch. "I'm due at practice

in about ten minutes. Maybe I should can it for the day and just tag along with you."

"No way," Elizabeth said. "Practice is important at this point."

"*You're* important."

"Don't worry." She gestured to Jessica. "We're going to the Braino tryouts. Then I'll go on to class. I'll be with somebody at virtually all times."

"I like that plan. But I also like the idea of me keeping an eye on you."

"Forget it," Elizabeth insisted. "If there's one thing I've had enough of, it's being followed around."

"You can do it," Denise said excitedly.

"No, I can't," Winston argued. "Look at that guy. He's knocking them dead."

There were twenty contestants, and Number Nineteen was winding up a tumbling routine that had the crowd roaring its approval.

"I'm going to withdraw," Winston announced, heading toward the bleacher on which a panel of twelve faculty members sat like Olympic judges. High up in the stands, an announcer read off the names of the contestants over a PA system.

Denise grabbed the back of Winston's shirt. "Oh no, you don't."

"Oh yes, I do."

"Not if you ever want to go out with me again," she said, lifting one eyebrow for emphasis.

"I was afraid you were going to say that," Winston croaked.

Number Nineteen finished his routine with a flourish and took a deep bow.

"Let's hear it for Frank Wright," urged the announcer over the loudspeaker.

The crowd cheered, and Winston noticed that every single member of the panel was smiling and applauding.

"And now," boomed the PA system, "please welcome Contestant Number Twenty, Winston Egbert."

There was a round of polite applause, and Winston felt a sense of cold, paralyzing dread. "I can't do it," he told Denise, backing up.

"What are you," Denise demanded, "a man or a mouse?"

"I'm an introvert."

"Since when?"

"Since now. Lets go."

"No! Now, get out there!" With that, Denise gave him a shove that sent him catapulting onto the field. The big shoes he wore crossed at the toes like skis, and his arms began to flail as he lost his balance.

"Yeeeooooow!" he cried, falling over backward.

"Flip!" he heard Denise yell from the sidelines.

Winston managed to turn the fall into a backward somersault. In the process, his wristwatch got stuck on a large button of his shirt. The result was a second backward somersault.

Unfortunately, one of the tips of his shoes got tangled in his suspenders, and by the time he rolled to a stop, he was a large, human knot. His arms and legs were hopelessly twisted together in a tangle of suspenders, buttons, sleeves, and oversized shoes.

"Ladies and gentlemen," he shouted to the audience. "The amazing Houdini will now extricate himself from . . . from . . . from . . . a pretty big mess."

The audience laughed and hooted.

Feeling a little better, Winston began to struggle, while the spectators in the bleachers roared. The longer he struggled, the harder they laughed.

Winston let out a long sigh and then ceased to struggle. He looked left. Then he looked right.

"Help!" he shrieked.

Denise came mincing out, wearing a borrowed Braino mask. When she reached the middle of the field, she held out the sides of her shorts and made a tiny curtsy. She began to "untie" Winston, removing his arms, legs, feet, and hands from their tangled positions.

When Denise was done, she executed a prim pirouette and took off with Winston's elasticized suspender accidentally on purpose caught on her bracelet.

Winston smiled at the audience, holding up his fingers and pretending to count from four to zero. Then he put his fingers in his ears when Denise came shooting back as if she'd been flung from a sling.

The crowd went wild.

"You're doing great," Denise said to Winston out of the side of her mouth.

"We're doing great," he corrected. "Don't leave me alone out here. We're a hit. Come on, let's both do the split routine—we'll pretend we're both stuck and can't get up."

The next ten minutes whizzed by like a dream. When the routine was over, they both stood up, took a bow, and then ran to the sidelines.

"The judges have made their decision," boomed the loudspeaker.

All the contestants froze, and Winston felt Denise reach for his hand.

"Due to popular demand, we'll be starting a

new Braino tradition. Congratulations to both Winston Egbert and Denise Waters!"

Denise let out a delighted whoop and jumped into Winston's waiting arms. The crowd stood up and gave them a standing ovation.

"As we all know, the upcoming game against State is the most important game of the season. As a gesture of team support and school solidarity, we'd like to encourage all Brainos to stay in costume until the game is over."

Once again, the crowd broke into laughter and applause.

"What do you know!" Winston exclaimed happily. "Today I got laughs *and* the girl."

Chapter
Ten

William jogged up the front steps of the Sweet Valley Hospital and glanced at his reflection in the glass door. The short brown wig he'd stolen from the costume room of the drama department looked fairly convincing. If somebody noticed him and was questioned later, they would give a fairly generalized description of a guy who could easily be Todd Wilkins.

William sauntered past the information desk and went directly to the elevator. *Room three twenty-four*, the operator had said when he'd called earlier.

The elevator doors opened and William stepped out onto the shiny linoleum floor. Except for a maintenance worker mopping at the far end of the hallway, there was no one in sight.

William walked softly down the corridor, reading the names on the doors. Carter. Golden. Vacant. Vacant. And then Steery. He turned the corner and came to an abrupt stop. The Nurses' Station loomed ahead.

An island in the center of a circular ward, the station was surrounded by activity. White-coated doctors, nurses, and technicians hurried in and out of rooms, often pausing briefly to glance at a chart or make a note. There was no way to slip past the station unnoticed.

William backed around the corner and watched the slow movements of the maintenance man. Narrowing his eyes, William sneaked up behind the worker. In a flash, he used his sharp elbow to hit his prey expertly over the back of the head.

His victim slumped, almost peacefully, into William's waiting arms. William quickly dragged the heavy body into one of the vacant rooms between Golden and Steery. He dumped the unconscious man on the bed and unzipped his loose orange coveralls. As he struggled to untangle the worker's limbs from his uniform, William's level of frustration rose to boiling point. By the time he finished the job, he was hot, irritable, and feeling so angry at Celine that he positively relished the prospect of finishing her off for good.

After slipping on the coveralls, he cautiously pressed his ear to the door. The sound of voices drifted in from the hallway. William took a deep breath, shot a last look at the sleeping man, and began whistling. Then he swung the door open and left the room with a confident gait. He smiled at two doctors who stood chatting next to the elevator as he walked past them and retrieved the abandoned mop and bucket.

Passing the doctors again as he made his way toward the Nurses' Station, William gave them another smile and nod. Both men reflexively returned his smile. They looked right through him, their conversation continuing in a steady stream.

William drenched the mop and swept it across the floor as he inched around the circular ward. He glanced up every few steps to read the names on the doors. *Ramos. Kelton. Barker.* BOUDREAUX!

He almost jumped when the door opened and a nurse and a doctor came walking out. They brushed past him, and William slipped inside the room before the door shut behind them.

Celine lay on a narrow bed, her eyes closed.

Without any makeup, she looked almost like a child. Her chest rose and fell in time to the rhythm of the humming respirator.

William removed the IV first, pulling the needle from her hand. Then he reached up to turn the dial on the respirator. He realized that killing Celine was going to be easy. Ridiculously easy.

"What do you think you're doing?"

William froze, and his head snapped in the direction of the door. A large male nurse stood in the doorway. He looked enraged and appalled. "Who are you?" he demanded, moving toward the bed. "Get away from that respirator!" he shouted menacingly.

William reached for the mop and held it over his head like a baseball bat. He let out a shout and swung it at the nurse's head. The man screamed and ducked down as the mop came whizzing over his head, missing him by centimeters. The mop hit a standing lamp, knocking it to the ground with a loud crash.

A red rage welled up in William. He longed to choke the life out of both Celine and the nurse. But there was no time. With all the noise, it was only a matter of seconds before reinforcements came barging in.

William vaulted over the nurse's stooping

152

figure and raced out the door, just as two female nurses arrived to investigate. He lowered his head as he bolted through them. He hit one in the stomach and thumped the other in the arm so hard that she let out a loud cry of pain.

William spotted a stairway just across the hall. He ran down the stairs, pulling off the coveralls as he went. When he reached the ground floor, he shoved the uniform underneath the concrete stairway. Then he removed the wig and stepped out into the hospital lobby.

He heard sirens coming close to the building and slowed to a walk. With a small smile, he took a seat on a nearby bench to watch the scene unfold. Five policemen jogged up the front steps and rushed past William. William stretched lazily, then strolled out of the hospital's double glass front doors.

"So you weren't upset when James Montgomery got thrown off the team?" Tom asked, pulling on his jersey.

"As far as I'm concerned, James is no loss," Pete Gleason replied. He put one foot on the bench and tightened his shoelace. "Sure, he was a good player. And at first, I didn't want to believe he was a bad guy. But I'm convinced he raped that girl, and I don't want a rapist for a teammate. Any guy who would do that . . ." Pete shook his head.

Jerry Carstairs shut his locker with a bang. "We're here to play football, and we're under a lot of pressure to win. Like it or not, if you punish Montgomery, you punish all of us. Is that fair? No way."

"You're saying James should have stayed on the team?" Tom asked.

"I'm saying the team *needs* James Montgomery," Jerry retorted angrily.

There was an uncomfortable silence. Jerry began to blush beet red and sputter in confusion. "Oh, wow! I don't . . . I'm sorry. I didn't mean that the way it came out. You're a great player, Tom. Everybody thinks you're a great player. We couldn't have a better substitute for James. No offense intended."

"None taken," Tom said kindly. "I'm interested in your opinion."

"I just think James is more useful to the school and to the community playing on this team than he is doing some social service project." He gave Tom a rueful smile. "The rest of us—I mean *you*," he said with emphasis, "have to pick up the slack."

"But you can't let a guy—or a girl, for that

matter—get away with a crime just because they're good at their job," Leroy Higgins argued.

George Perkins adjusted a piece of padding in his helmet. "I agree with Leroy and Pete."

"I think most people, including me, agree with Leroy and Pete," Mo Bentley, the student assistant coach, said. "College athletic organizations have to weed out the bad guys. Some people think getting rid of team members is bad for morale, but really, it's good. Don't you like knowing that you're part of a team that takes a position on what's right and wrong? I do."

A couple of guys who'd been listening to the conversation as they dressed rolled their eyes.

"OK. OK. Maybe it sounds a little preachy. But from a practical standpoint, it's in our best interest. If you stick up for a guy who you know is doing something wrong just because he's your teammate, then you won't have any credibility—and neither will your team."

The sound of a whistle out on the field spurred everyone to action. There was a series of echoing clangs as each player grabbed his helmet and slammed his locker shut.

Tom fell into step beside Mo. "So you think morale is good?" he asked.

Mo nodded. "I do. And I think having Tom Watts rejoin the team has done a lot to boost enthusiasm." Mo gave him a friendly punch in the arm.

Tom felt a momentary flicker of worry. Had he compromised the integrity of his story by becoming too much a part of it? He was supposed to be objectively reporting on the morale of the team, not exerting an influence over it.

He wished that producer, Bob, would call him so he could talk about his angle on the story. Tom sighed. More than anything, he wished he could talk about it with Elizabeth, too. Worry nagged at his brain. When he finally told Elizabeth the whole truth about why he'd rejoined the football team, she wasn't going to be happy. Elizabeth hated it when he kept anything from her.

But maybe her reporter's instincts would prevail. She'd understand that he'd been asked to work undercover in pursuit of a story—and that's exactly what he'd done.

The piece was shaping up nicely. With a little luck, SVU would win the game against State, and the story would have a spectacular and climactic ending.

He made a note to himself to remind Farley

from the station to shoot some locker-room footage. Postgame interviews always added a good touch of color to a television sports piece. Even if the VideoNet deal didn't happen, WSVU would still want to do a piece on the game.

The whole campus was psyched to see SVU play against State. There was a palpable excitement in the air. Although William White's suicide and the Todd Wilkins/Celine Boudreaux story had cast a pall over the enthusiasm, the student body seemed particularly energized. In a way, the tragedy added an interesting element to his piece. The story wasn't just about the *team's* postscandal morale, it was about the whole campus. An entire student body trying to cope with a series of shattering scandals and hideous crimes.

Maybe he really would wind up with a piece on the national news. William White's incarceration had certainly made all the front pages. That kind of high-profile tie-in might be just the hook he needed to grab the national spotlight.

Tom came to an abrupt halt and felt suddenly sick to his stomach. What kind of a low-life tabloid parasite was he turning into? He'd actually been thinking about how he could sensationalize human tragedy for personal gain. Even worse, it was tragedy that had struck uncomfortably close to home.

There were a lot of threads weaving this story together, he realized. And they all led back to the same person.

Elizabeth.

William White had tried to murder Elizabeth. Todd Wilkins had tried to murder Celine Boudreaux—and had been stalking Elizabeth. James Montgomery had tried to rape Jessica, Elizabeth's sister.

Tom shivered from head to foot. There was some very weird karma in the air. Was there something he was missing? Something he wasn't seeing?

"Anything wrong?" Mo asked.

"I just had a chill, that's all," Tom answered.

Moe looked slightly alarmed. "You're not getting sick, are you?"

"No way."

"Good. Because we're counting on you." Mo slapped Tom on the back, then stuck his whistle into his mouth and ran across the field, signaling the defensive ends to line up.

Tom looked around the empty stands. There was something slightly sinister about the vast, empty stadium. He had the feeling that somewhere up there somebody was watching.

And waiting.

"Elizabeth!" Alexandra called, panting. "Elizabeth, wait."

Several yards ahead, Elizabeth stopped and turned.

Alexandra gulped in air, trying to catch her breath. She felt as if she'd been running for the past hour. "I've been looking for you everywhere. Have you heard the news?"

"What news?"

"Todd turned up at the hospital and made another attempt to murder Celine."

The color drained from Elizabeth's face, and she dropped her books.

Alexandra leaned over to retrieve them. "I went back to my room after the Braino tryouts and heard it on the radio. Apparently, he tried to unhook her respirator."

"Did they arrest him?"

Alexandra shook her head. "No. He attacked a nurse and ran out. The police have put out an all-points bulletin."

"An APB for Todd?" Elizabeth asked, her voice full of shock and disbelief.

She rubbed her forehead and then ran her

hand down over her face. "I feel like I'm about to lose my mind."

"I thought you should know what was going on," Alexandra said. "Liz, I'm worried about you."

"Well, I'm worried about Todd," Elizabeth replied, sounding almost angry. "This is Todd we're talking about. *Todd Wilkins*. The more I think about it, the less sense it makes. Todd has always been fair, compassionate, kind, and—until recently—even-tempered. I'm having a hard time believing he could do all the things that he's been accused of."

"The police sure seem to believe it. And what about the dolls and the notes?"

Elizabeth sat down on a bench. "I can't help but wonder if there isn't another explanation."

Alexandra sighed heavily and sat down next to Elizabeth. "I don't know what to think anymore either. Todd used to be a great guy, but now . . ." She trailed off and shrugged. "Let's face it. Ever since he started drinking, he hasn't been the same."

"Has he ever tried to hurt you?"

Alexandra bit her lip. "No. Mainly, he just acted like a jerk."

"There's a big difference between being a jerk and being a crazed murderer. All my instincts and all my brains are telling me that Todd Wilkins is not capable of murder. Do you, in your heart of hearts, disagree?"

Alexandra looked around. There were tall trees and shadows everywhere. Someone could be hiding in a thousand different places. "Why can't you just be careful until they find Todd and figure out just exactly what's going on?" Alexandra demanded, suddenly furious. "Why are you so determined to make it harder than it already is on the people who care about you?"

Elizabeth's lip began to tremble. "Please don't start on me," she begged.

"I don't want to sound mean. But Elizabeth, come on. Tom's worried. Jessica is worried. I'm worried. We care about you, and if you cared about us you'd take some commonsense precautions."

"I *am* being cautious," Elizabeth protested.

"Then prove it," Alexandra said. She turned on her heel and began stalking off. She'd done her duty. She had told Elizabeth that Todd was still loose and considered dangerous. *If Elizabeth chooses not to believe it, that's her decision,* she resolved. *But I'm through worrying about it.*

*   *   *

"I thought you were through worrying about it," Noah said gently. "You've done everything you can. If Elizabeth doesn't want to be cautious, you can't control that."

"I can't quit thinking about her. I have a gut feeling that something terrible is going to happen."

It was late afternoon, and Alexandra and Noah were sitting in Noah's room listening to the radio for updated reports on Todd. The quarterly newscast had just ended with a reiteration of what had been broadcast earlier. Todd was still at large.

Alexandra leaned over and turned down the volume. "I don't know what to think. I listen to the radio, and I hear that Todd Wilkins is wanted for attempted murder—and I believe it. I listen to Elizabeth and start thinking she's right—Todd could never do something like that." She rolled over on her side and propped her head up on her elbow. "You're a psychology major. What do you think?"

Noah blew out his breath and ran his hands through his hair. "I'm just a sophomore psych major. Not an expert on the criminally insane."

Alexandra sat up and groaned. "I can't stand this level of stress. The drama is driving me crazy."

"Really?" Noah asked in a surprised tone. There was an odd note in his voice.

"What do you mean, *really*?" Alexandra asked curiously.

Noah shrugged. "I don't know. I wondered if maybe the . . . *drama* of all this was exciting to you."

Alexandra sat up a little straighter. "I have the feeling I've been insulted. Could you explain that remark?"

"I'm not trying to insult you. I'm just expressing a concern."

"A concern that I get my kicks from cheap thrills?"

"No, of course not."

"That I like seeing my friends in danger?"

"No!" Noah cried in a defensive tone. "I'm not going about this the right way. I was really trying to express a worry that I have about myself, not one that I have about you. Well, I guess it *is* a concern about you. I'm concerned that you might react to this concern I have about myself and . . ."

"What are you talking about?" Alexandra interrupted.

"Do you think I'm dull?" he blurted out.

"Dull?"

"Yeah. I'm afraid I'm dull—as in boring," he

said simply. "I'm not like the rest of your friends. I don't seem to wind up in dramatic situations or have a lot of major problems. And I can't remember the last time I had a crisis. Well, I did have to have an emergency root canal a couple of months ago, but . . ."

Alexandra doubled over and fell backward.

"Are you laughing at me, or did you just have a sudden attack of appendicitis?"

"I'm laughing at you," she said, wheezing. She gazed at his slightly bewildered face and smiled. "Noah. That's exactly what I like about you. You're steady, stable . . ." She opened her hands, trying to find the right words. "You're . . . you're . . ."

"Dull?" he suggested helpfully.

"No. Never dull. Dependable. That's it. You're dependable. I feel like I can count on you. I can trust you."

He gave her a crooked smile. "Then can I count on you not to get bored with me?"

"I could never get bored with you." Alexandra leaned forward and gently kissed him on the cheek.

This just in, a faint voice announced on the radio.

Alexandra and Noah broke apart, and Noah turned up the sound.

Police have informed Station WZBH that Todd Wilkins is believed to still be in the Sweet Valley University area. Students and residents are advised to be alert and on the lookout for a young white male, nineteen years old, with short brown hair and brown eyes. He was last seen wearing orange coveralls. If you see this man, call the police immediately. He's dangerous and possibly armed.

Alexandra stood up and began pacing restlessly with her arms across her chest. "I just don't know what to do. I don't know what to think. I don't know what to expect."

"That's pretty comprehensive," Noah commented, standing up too.

"I wish you were an expert on criminal insanity," Alexandra sighed.

"Unfortunately, I'm not." Suddenly, he snapped his fingers. "But I know of someone who is."

"*Make 'em laugh. Make 'em laugh.*" It was the third time Winston and Denise had lip-synched the famous song from *Singing in the Rain*. They stood in front of the full-length mirror that hung on the door of Winston's room. As they launched into their grand finale, Winston thought they looked as glamorous as Debbie Reynolds and Gene Kelly.

He leaned forward and swung his arms back and forth while moonwalking with his feet. He appeared to be executing a very demanding dance step.

Denise began to giggle. "Show me how to do that. We could turn this into a funny routine and do it at the game." She reached for her Braino mask and pulled it on.

Never, in the whole course of their relationship, had Winston felt so close to Denise. *I'm in love,* his heart thumped in time to the music.

"Ta-da!" sang Denise, striking a final pose and blowing kisses at an imaginary audience.

Winston popped the CD out of the player. "Did you enjoy being a clown today?"

She considered the question for a long time. "Winston, it was, without a doubt, the biggest rush I've ever experienced."

"Now you know. Now you understand."

"Understand what?"

"What makes a class clown the class clown. The attention. The laughter. It's like the most exhilarating feeling in the world. And it's safe."

"Safe how?"

"When you're a clown, you're always behind makeup. You can take risks, because if you say something dumb, or do something that

166

backfires, you can always laugh and say you were kidding."

"I know what you mean about risk," Denise agreed. "I felt like I was really working without a net today. I've never had any performing experience at all. I jumped in there today to try to save you and . . . and . . . I don't know what happened. The minute I felt the audience respond to what I was doing, I just had to keep going."

"We worked well together," he said. "Your instincts for comedy are great."

"That's because I've been dating you for so long." She happily honked her big red nose.

She honked it again, and Winston thought he'd never heard a sweeter sound. "I can't believe I'm really part of this Braino thing," she sighed happily.

"Me neither," Winston smiled. "It's like . . . I don't know . . . we finally have something in common." He put on his own Braino mask and stood beside her, staring again at their reflections in the mirror.

"We've always had things in common," Denise said.

"Name one," Winston challenged.

"Well, we both like to eat. *But* I like spicy food, and you like bland food. That doesn't mean anything, though. We have other things in common."

"No, we don't," Winston argued. "I like classic rock. You like heavy metal and New Age. You like documentaries, I like action adventure."

"Well . . ." Denise hesitated.

"Face it. You say potato and I say po-tah-to . . ." Winston sang off-key.

"If you're leading up to calling this whole thing off . . ." Denise began.

"I'm leading up to let's get married," Winston said, his heart hammering in his chest. There. It was finally out. He'd popped the question.

He'd thought long and hard about this all day, not sure he would work up the nerve to ask her. But he knew he loved Denise more than anything else in the world. And he wanted to know she loved him back.

Winston reached behind his desk and pulled out a cardboard sign he'd made: JUST MARRIED. "We could put this on the back of the Brainmobile."

Denise let out a peal of laughter. "Wouldn't that be a hoot? I could wear a veil over the mask. A long, flowing veil that would stream out about six yards." She began to pace around. "I'll have a bouquet of those silly clown flowers that squirt water. This will be so cool." Denise took off her mask and threw back her head. Her laughter was deep and rich.

Winston's heart sank. Obviously, she wasn't going to take him seriously. He caught a glimpse of himself in the mirror and realized he couldn't blame her. No girl wanted to receive a marriage proposal from a guy in a rubber mask. Even a clown was expected to get down on one knee, produce a ring, and pop the question while a guy with a mustache and a violin played something romantic in the background.

Denise frowned suddenly. "Oh, shoot. I just remembered I can't drive to the game with you in the Brainmobile."

"Why not?" Winston demanded.

"I really need to ride in the van with Jessica. Isabella called me, and we both agreed that with all the stuff that's been going on, Jessica *and* Elizabeth need lots of support."

"What about me?" he yipped. "Don't you think *I* need support?"

"I'll have to take my Braino gear with me," Denise murmured to herself, paying no attention.

"I want you to ride with me," he persisted. "I'm supposed to meet Mark Janos tonight to get the keys to theBrainmobile."

"Where *is* the Brainmobile between gigs?" Denise asked absently, her mind obviously racing off in several different directions.

"On the bottom level of the garage under Marsden," Winston replied. "Denise," he whimpered, "I want you to ride with me. You're supposed to be Mrs. Braino, remember?"

She put a fond hand on his cheek. "I'll ride with you on the way back. How 'bout that? Oh, wow! Look at what time it is. I've got to get to the Theta house. I promised Isabella I'd help make some cookies to take to the game." Denise picked up her purse and her jacket. She paused at the door and seemed to notice, for the first time, the forlorn, unhappy look on his face. "Winston?" she said in a curious tone. "You *were* joking, right? I mean, about getting married?"

Winston cleared his throat and nervously licked his lips. Should he say no? Tell her he had never been more serious in his whole life? That's what he wanted to do.

But it was a risk. A big risk. Sure, she might drop her stuff and throw herself into his arms. She might promise to marry him and love him forever.

On the other hand, she might just laugh

and say no. No for real. No for now. And no for always. That was more risk than he was ready to take.

This proposal had backfired, and it was time to backpedal. "Serious? Me? Nahhhh! I was just kidding."

Chapter Eleven

Danny fumbled slightly with the key as he hurried to get his door open before the phone stopped ringing. His backpack hung over one shoulder, and he gripped his jacket under his arm. A bag of take-out dangled precariously from one finger.

He could hear the phone ring again and again. Finally, he managed to jiggle the key and shove the door open. "Hello?" he said breathlessly, struggling to get the phone up to his ear while he gingerly placed his food bag on the desk and let his jacket drop to the floor.

"Hey, Danny. It's Tim. How's it going?"

Danny grinned, letting his backpack slide down his arm and drop to the floor next to his jacket. "Like clockwork. I called Sweet Valley

Auto Rentals, and everybody's agreed to chip in for the minivan."

"Great. Great. So who's *everybody*? All of Tom's good buddies and buddettes?"

Danny pulled his chair up to the desk and sat down. "That's right."

"So how're you going to work this so Tom doesn't find out?"

"The team bus leaves from Marsden, and the charter buses that take students leave from the stadium parking lot. We've worked it out so we won't be anywhere near those buses. I've told everybody to meet me in the parking lot behind Dickenson Hall."

"Sounds good, so far." Danny could hear the satisfaction in Tim's voice.

"Winston Egbert—the guy who's the new Braino—is going to help. I'll pick up the minivan early in the morning and park it under Marsden with the Brainmobile. As soon as Winston sees the team bus leave, he'll drive the minivan around to Dickenson, leave it, and then catch up with us later in the Brainmobile."

"Wow!" Tim whistled his admiration. "You thought this thing through like a pro. Ever think about coaching? We can always use a good strategist."

Danny laughed.

"You guys will take him back to campus with you in the van, I guess."

"Sure," Danny said. "I figured we'd all go to dinner after the game."

"That sounds nice. Really, really nice. Listen, Danny," Tim said, his voice turning serious, "I really want to thank you. Tomorrow is going to be quite an event in the life of Tom Watts, and it couldn't have happened without you."

"Hi, Braino."

"Bye, Braino."

"Yo! Braino."

Jessica looked around at the crowd of students who'd gathered in the quad. It looked like a Braino convention. Ever since the tryouts this morning, SVU had broken out in Braino fever. There were Brainos everywhere, and the atmosphere was like a masked ball. Jessica had been the recipient of a lot of flirtatious compliments from familiar voices.

"Hello, beautiful," a Braino said to Jessica as he politely stood aside to let her pass. Jessica pressed her lips together to keep from laughing. She recognized that voice. It belonged to the adenoidal, dweeby guy who sat behind her in Physics. Normally, he was so shy and nervous around Jessica that he practically began hyperventilating if she said hello. Now that he had a mask on, he was a regular Romeo.

"This is going to be great," she heard one girl behind her say to another. "The SVU stands are going to look great. Did you get a Braino mask?"

"No," the second girl answered in an unhappy voice. "The bookstore is sold out. It's Brainomania."

Jessica veered off the sidewalk and crossed the wooded area on her way to the dorm. It had been a busy afternoon. Classes. A quick visit to the Theta house. She'd had to answer sixty million questions about Todd and her sister.

She quickened her step, eager to get back to her room and check on Elizabeth. There was no one on the sidewalk now, and Jessica was aware of an almost eerie silence.

Her heart began to thud a bit faster, and a series of morbid, gory pictures flashed through her mind.

A bloody, decapitated Ken doll.

Two broken and twisted Barbie dolls.

Celine Boudreaux lying in a hospital bed.

The hair on the back of her neck stood up when Jessica heard shuffling sounds behind her. She tried to proceed quietly, listening. There were definitely footsteps behind her. She wanted to scream, but instead she summoned all her courage and whirled around. She let out her breath with a long, whistling sigh of relief.

Ambling along the sidewalk behind her was just another Braino. He gave Jessica an acknowledging smile and nod, then continued walking with his head down.

"I'm totally losing it," Jessica muttered to herself. "What kind of nitwit gets spooked by a Braino?"

Just before Jessica disappeared inside the front door of her dorm, she turned and gave him a little wave.

William smiled and waved back.

This Braino business was a stroke of luck, he reflected. He couldn't have come up with a better plan for moving undetected around the campus.

His mind lingered briefly on his failed attempt to murder Céline. He thrust his hand into the pocket of the windbreaker he'd stolen from the cafeteria and squeezed the neck of one of the dolls he was carrying. Celine would have to be dealt with. But there would be time for that later.

Perhaps Elizabeth, once she realized the enormous lengths to which he'd gone to procure her love and undivided attention, would even consent to help him.

She was going to be angry at first—that was to be expected. In time she would get over it.

But seeing Jessica had made William think about something.

Elizabeth was very fond of her sister. If, because of any scheme of William's, something *unfortunate* were to happen to Jessica, Elizabeth would be very upset with him.

She might even be so upset she'd refuse to help him tie up the few loose ends that would remain after tomorrow's big game. So upset she wouldn't want to leave the country with him.

He watched the dorm with narrow eyes. Hmmmm. This called for a little plan adjustment.

A group of girls passed him by, hurrying up the walk to the dorm. He looked at his watch. There was still one more class period today, which probably meant that there was still a fair amount of coming and going in the halls.

William paused. He had a message to leave Elizabeth, and he didn't want anyone to find it before she did. Perhaps he shouldn't enter Dickenson Hall until the dinner hour had begun.

He pivoted sharply and began hurrying back toward the main part of the campus. Elizabeth's last class was English Lit. He'd wait for her outside the building and then follow her home.

He'd make sure she arrived safe and sound. And then give her the message.

Again, we have no new information. Todd Wilkins is apparently still on or near the Sweet Valley University campus, and police are continuing their search. There are no clues as to his whereabouts at this time, but anyone having information should immediately contact the Sweet Valley Police.

The newscaster's drone was replaced by the upbeat voice of the DJ as he announced the return to top-forty programming.

Todd watched the driver of the blue VW that sat parked in the alley turn off the radio when the back door to the La Noche restaurant opened.

A young woman came hurrying out, balling up an apron and tossing it into a hamper that stood outside the door. She jumped into the VW and gave the driver a kiss. The car pulled out of the parking lot and peeled off down the street.

Todd carefully stepped out from behind a Dumpster and headed south toward campus. He'd taken every back street and alley in town in order to avoid being spotted by the police.

He wished he knew what was going on. This was a nightmare. A surreal, horrible nightmare from which he half expected to awaken drenched with sweat.

When he reached the street that ran behind the dormitories, he stepped behind a line of tall bushes at the edge of campus and peered out.

If he could just find Elizabeth and explain what was going on, maybe she could help him somehow. She could convince the police that he was innocent. And help him figure out who was behind this elaborate plot to destroy him.

A group of laughing students came out the front door of Dickenson and headed toward the quad. Three of the five girls were wearing Braino masks.

Todd scratched his head. Why so many people walking around in Braino masks? He'd seen several kids in masks near the parking lot and a bunch of people in full Braino costume on the other side of the campus.

He caught his breath when he saw Elizabeth coming up the walkway toward the dorm. He started to step out from his hiding place but froze when he saw a male Braino walking several yards behind her. Todd stepped back farther into the bushes. He couldn't afford to scare

Elizabeth and have her start screaming at him again. The Braino guy would either jump him or call for help. Either way, Todd would never get a chance to talk to Elizabeth.

He watched her disappear into the building and squatted down to wait until the Braino followed her a couple of minutes later.

Todd waited several minutes, then emerged from the bushes and hurried up the walk. He ducked inside the door, grateful that the lobby was empty. He quickly climbed the steps to Elizabeth's floor.

Elizabeth's room was just around the corner. As he approached the door, he squinted. There was something on the floor in front of her door. Something that looked like . . .

He blinked and stepped closer, bending down to examine the ugly scene made with hideous dolls. He leaned down to look at a note that had been place with the dolls. *"Soon, I will be the only one left in your life. I will be everything to you, just as you are everything to me. The others will be destroyed."*

Todd sat back on his heels, his mind racing. He remembered Elizabeth standing in his dorm room with her arms crossed over her chest.

"I want to talk to you about what's been going on."

"I didn't steal the car."

"I'm not talking about the car. I'm talking about the stuff you left in my room."

"What stuff?"

"The dolls. . . . I know it's you. And I want it to stop."

Now he understood. Somebody had been harassing her for a while. No wonder she was so jumpy. He stood and accidentally jostled the pile of dolls. They thumped against the door. Todd backed away, his eyes glued to the door. If she looked out and saw him, there was no telling what she might do.

"Did you hear something outside?" Jessica asked.

Elizabeth nodded. "Yeah, I think so." She moved toward the door with her heart in her throat.

Jessica picked up the phone to go through her Security routine again. "Ready. Set. Open," she urged.

Elizabeth pulled the door open and then jumped and shrieked when something fell against her toe.

Jessica screamed, too, and dropped the phone.

Elizabeth slammed the door and one of the

dolls caught in the hinges. A smear of fresh red paint, like blood, stained the floor and the toe of Elizabeth's white sneaker. She shouted, struggling to slam the door but unable to make it shut. "Help me," she wept, terrified. "Help."

The next thing she knew, Jessica was at her elbow, prying her fingers from the doorknob. "Let go!" she was yelling. "Let go, or it won't close."

Elizabeth fell back, and Jessica quickly scooped in the grotesque pile of dolls with her foot. Then she slammed the door and turned the lock.

While Jessica hurried to the bureau and began shoving it in front of the door, Elizabeth bent down and studied the pile of Barbie and Ken dolls that lay twisted, broken, and splattered with red paint. A note was attached to the back of a Ken doll wearing a football helmet. With a shaking hand, Elizabeth removed the note and read aloud. "'Soon, I will be the only one left in your life. I will be everything to you, just as you are everything to me.'"

Jessica put their desk chairs in front of the bureau for good measure, then dusted her hands and reached out to take the note.

Elizabeth handed it to her and replaced the telephone receiver. Two seconds later, it rang.

She and Jessica exchanged an agonized look.

"Go ahead," Jessica whispered. "Answer it."

Elizabeth picked up the receiver as if it were a snake. "Hello?"

"It's me. Todd. Don't say anything, please. Just let me talk."

"Is it him?" Jessica mouthed.

Elizabeth nodded at her.

"You're in danger, Liz. But not from me. Probably from the same guy who's been ruining my life. Somebody's got it in for both of us."

Elizabeth felt the muscles in her neck and jaw tightening. So far, she had taken the position that Todd wasn't capable of murder. She'd thought that his downward spiral was due to alcohol and a series of tough breaks.

But so far, she hadn't considered the possibility that he was truly insane. Paranoid, delusional, and insane.

She took a deep breath and forced herself to calm down and think clearly. "I think you're right," she said, trying to keep the fear out of her voice. "I think I am in danger. And I'd like to talk to you about it. Where are you? If you tell me, I'll come and meet you."

"Todd? Will you tell me where you are?"

With a sinking heart, Todd realized she

184

didn't believe him. She thought he wanted to hurt her. She thought he was a threat.

"Todd? Please tell me where I can find you."

There was fear in her voice. And she was using a patronizing tone that most people reserved for small children who were behaving irrationally. He'd also heard that strange, pleasant, but strained voice used on insane people. *Lunatics.*

"Todd? Todd, it would be so much easier if we could meet face-to-face."

Fighting despair, he replaced the receiver and leaned against the inside wall of the phone booth. With his back to the street, he was safely hidden from the view of passersby.

What should he do now? Whom could he turn to? Who could help him?

The answer was nobody.

You're on your own, Wilkins, a little voice inside his head said. *It's time to quit whining and sneaking around. Take charge of this situation. Take control of your life—what's left of it.*

He hung his head. Somebody had framed him twice. Although he didn't know why or how they'd done it, Todd did know that he'd made it easy for them to do it. Lounging around campus like a bum. Crawling into the bottle. He'd been acting like a creep in a thousand different ways. No wonder people believed he was capable of car theft and murder. If only he'd kept his head held high in the weeks following the sports scandal and weathered the storms with his chin up and his character intact. Then he'd be dealing from a position of strength right now, instead of slinking around and *feeling* like a guilty criminal.

Todd slid the door to the phone booth open and looked around. There were a few people around, but nobody seemed to be looking straight at him. Todd walked out standing tall.

Elizabeth thought *he* was the big danger. That meant she was going to be on her guard—but against the wrong person. She was more vulnerable than she realized. He'd tried to warn her but failed. Now the only way to protect her was to find out who was at the root of all this.

He and Elizabeth went back a long way. He owed her whatever protection he could manage. And he owed it to himself and his family to clear his name and put his life back together.

He mentally reviewed their respective lists of friends and potential enemies and came up blank. He couldn't come up with anyone who would be sick enough to go to these lengths.

Who could it be? Who?

Todd closed his eyes and conjured up a mental picture of Elizabeth, imagining the way she had looked earlier today. Her blond hair had been flying out behind her. . . .

"Braino!" he said out loud, stopping in his tracks. There had been a Braino walking behind Elizabeth. And he'd walked right into Dickenson Hall behind her. Whoever left the dolls had only had a matter of seconds in which to arrange them. It must have been the Braino—no one else had gone inside.

He had a trembling sense of excitement—almost like an awakening. Todd's mind was finally starting to operate again, and he couldn't wait to use it.

Obviously, he needed to make himself inconspicuous. Todd smiled for the first time in days. He realized that if he wanted to follow Elizabeth, and move around campus without being noticed, putting on a Braino mask was a pretty good way to do it.

If it worked for the psycho who'd followed Elizabeth to her room today, it would work for Todd, too.

He slipped into the front door of Marsden Hall and moved down the hall until he saw an open door. Quickly, Todd peeked inside.

Bingo. Sitting on a nightstand next to the bed was exactly what he'd been hoping to find.

He reached out and grabbed it.

I've never stolen anything in my life, dammit, he heard his shrill, hysterical voice protesting to the police officer.

Well, there's a first time for everything, he reflected ruefully. Todd pulled the Braino mask down over his face and ducked back into the hall.

Chapter Twelve

"Thank you for seeing me, doctor . . ."

"Call me Jules," the older man said, breezing into the office. He gave Noah's hand a friendly shake and gestured for him to sit.

Noah smiled. "Thank you." He settled himself into a deep armchair. "I know it's late, and you're probably ready to go home, and . . ."

The doctor sat down behind his desk and shook his head in a dismissive fashion. "No apologies necessary. After the escape and suicide of one of our patients, there's been a lot of extra work. I'm spending most nights here in case I'm needed. Something like that is very upsetting to the other patients."

"Yeah!" Noah said. "I guess it would be."

"Now, what can I do for you, young man? I understand you attended one of my lectures at

SVU and are here seeking advice." He smiled, his tired eyes crinkling. "Not on your own behalf, I assume. You appear to be quite sane."

Noah didn't know whether or not he should laugh. He'd never talked to a psychiatrist before, and he was a little nervous about it. Was the doctor being serious? If so, he might think Noah was being weird if he laughed. On the other hand, he might think he was abnormal if he *didn't* laugh.

It was probably better to err on the side of serious. "I am sane," Noah said quickly. "At least, I'm pretty sure I am." He frowned. "If I weren't, would I know it?"

The doctor chuckled and leaned back in his chair. Noah relaxed a bit. Obviously, the doctor had a sense of humor. "I'm more or less convinced that we're all insane," the doctor said, stretching the muscles of his neck. "It's just a question of degree."

"But how do we know if someone is *criminally* insane?" Noah asked.

The doctor's smile abruptly disappeared, and he met Noah's eyes squarely. "Perhaps you'd better tell me what brought you here."

"This isn't about me, really. It's about a friend." Noah felt himself blush a fiery red. "I know everybody says that, but it's true. I have a friend whose old boyfriend is stalking her. He's doing really bizarre things, and none of us know how seriously to take him. We don't know how to gauge if he's really a threat."

"Has he made any serious attempt to harm her or anyone else?"

Noah nodded grimly. "He's the guy who tried to kill Celine Boudreaux, the SVU student. Then tried to finish her off in the hospital."

The doctor sat forward. His tired eyes had widened, and he reached for a notepad. He looked alert and very, very concerned.

"The thing is, Elizabeth—my friend—thinks that he wouldn't hurt her because they've been friends for so long."

Noah described in as much detail as he could the dolls, the notes, and all the other strange stunts Todd had pulled. "So what do you think?" he asked finally. "Is Elizabeth in danger?"

"I think that your friend should exercise every precaution until this boy is apprehended by the police. Is he capable of criminally violent behavior? Obviously. Is he capable of harming her? There's no way I can make a judgment about that without talking to Mr. Wilkins. Even then"—he shrugged, lifting his glasses and tapping them against his palm—"psychiatry is, at best, a very inexact science. I do know this: It's

191

impossible to predict with any certainty what *any* human being will do. The sane as well as the unbalanced."

He dropped his glasses on the desk and stood up, massaging his temples with an unhappy expression on his face. "There was a young woman who worked here. An orderly. She absolutely should have known that she needed to be on her guard with our patients every single second. Yet unbeknownst to me, she developed a relationship with William White. As a result, she's now dead."

Noah felt a chill run up his spine. Suddenly, he was impatient to get back to campus; he needed to warn Elizabeth and Alexandra. He stood up and extended his hand. "I think you've answered my questions. I really appreciate your seeing me."

"Call me anytime. I mean it." The doctor took Noah's arm and walked him out the door and down the hall. He removed a key from his pocket and unlocked a door that led to another hallway. "Just follow this hall. When you get to the door, buzz the attendant on the other side. He'll let you out."

"Thanks again," Noah said. The door shut behind him with a firm click.

There was a thick pad under the hall carpet,

and Noah noticed the walls were covered with a vinyl surface. When he reached out to touch it, the wall felt spongy. The whole place appeared to be padded.

At the end of the hall was a heavy, locked door. Noah bypassed the buzzer and instead knocked politely on the door's thick glass inset. The attendant on the other side glanced up and frowned. It wasn't the same attendant who had been on duty when he had come in. Obviously, the guy wasn't expecting anyone to be coming out.

"I'm a visitor," Noah shouted through the door. "Would you let me out, please?"

"Is your name on the list?" The attendant picked up a clipboard and studied it.

"It should be. Noah Pearson."

"OK," the attendant said, nodding as he found the information. "You're right here." He read from the page. "Noah Pearson, here to see Dr. Hemphill."

"All right! I'm convinced. Believe me, I'm convinced."

"So you'll ask the police for protection? And let Tom know exactly what's going on?" Jessica pressed.

"I will," Elizabeth said. "But not yet. Not until tomorrow after the game. Tom's got enough to worry about. I don't want him to know about the last batch of dolls. And I don't want him to know what Dr. Hemphill told Noah. It might throw him off balance and affect the way he plays."

"Elizabeth!" Jessica began. "Why do you always have to be so stubborn?"

"And why do you always have to be so selfless?" Alexandra demanded irritably. "It's like you've got some kind of martyr complex."

"Hey!" Elizabeth said angrily. "If you two are going to gang up on me, then I'm leaving."

"You're not going anywhere," Jessica snorted. "It's dark."

"I'm not going out by myself, either," Alexandra said. "Noah's going to come over and walk me back to my room."

Jessica flopped on her bed and gave them both a droopy look. "You guys are lucky, you know."

"Yeah!" Elizabeth said sourly. "I can't tell you how lucky I feel. I love knowing that one of my oldest friends has become a crazed lunatic and is out there waiting to kill me."

"There's also a guy out there who wants to protect you, and be with you, and hold you," she sighed. "Alexandra's got a guy like that, too. How did you guys know how to pick them? I always wind up with such duds."

"Things haven't always been great between Tom and me," Elizabeth said, hugging her knees and resting her chin on them. "We got off to a very bumpy start."

"Ditto for Noah and me," Alexandra said, laughing. "Actually, we had a great relationship before we'd ever met."

"Huh?" Jessica and Elizabeth looked at her blankly.

Alexandra told them the story of how earlier in the semester, when she'd been having some problems, she'd called the campus hot line. She'd spoken anonymously with an amazing crisis counselor, and they'd had long conversations almost every day. At the same time, Alexandra and Noah had met in their psychology class and developed crushes on each other. When Noah finally figured that she was the girl who'd been calling, they realized that they'd already gotten through the initial getting-to-know-each-other phase. "Can you believe it?" Alexandra laughed. "It was like something out of a movie."

"That's a great story. You should do something with it," Elizabeth suggested. "It would make a great play."

"You're the writer," Alexandra reminded her.

"Maybe it's something we could work on together," Elizabeth said.

"Maybe so." Alexandra smiled and dropped her eyes, feeling suddenly awkward and self-conscious. She and Elizabeth were finally repairing some of their damaged friendship. Even if they would never be *best* friends again—the way they had been in high school—at least they could be close.

"Thank you for having Noah get all that information," Elizabeth said, as if reading her thoughts. "I really appreciate it. And I appreciate the way you've kept us company." She laughed. "Not too many people want to drop by to see you when they know a homicidal maniac may be lurking around the place."

"The downstairs doors are locked at night," Jessica reminded Elizabeth. "As long as we keep our door locked tonight, we'll be safe."

"So tell me about your bumpy start with Tom," Alexandra said, trying to divert their minds from Todd.

Elizabeth crossed her arms and twisted her mouth. "I'm more concerned with our bumpy ending. After the game, when he finds out that I didn't tell him the whole truth about what's been going on with Todd, he's probably going to be really mad at me."

"So launch a preemptive strike," Jessica suggested.

"What do you mean?"

"Do something incredibly thoughtful for him. Something that will make him feel like he doesn't have any right to get mad at you, because you've been so nice to him."

"That's pretty devious," Elizabeth said.

"Yeah. But it's smart," Alexandra commented. "Let's think of something."

Elizabeth snapped her fingers and went to her desk. "I know. If I still have the . . ." She opened a drawer and rummaged around. "Aha!" She triumphantly held up a plastic packet.

"What's that?"

"Foil letters." She sat down on the floor and began spreading them out. "Let's see, do I have enough? Yes. I think I do." Elizabeth quickly rearranged the letters, with Jessica and Alexandra looking over her shoulder.

"'Good luck, Tom. Love, Liz,'" Alexandra read out loud.

"I'll take them over to Winston tomorrow morning. I can ask him to display the letters from the back of the Brammobile."

"I'll do that," Jessica offered. "You stay here and help Danny get everything organized. You're better at that than I am—and it'll be safer."

"What makes you think *you'll* be safe running

over to the Marsden garage?" Elizabeth demanded.

"Todd's not stalking me," Jessica pointed out. "And it'll be broad daylight."

There was a knock on the door. "It's Noah. Are you ready?"

Alexandra grabbed her purse and her jacket and stood. "I'll see you guys tomorrow."

Jessica and Elizabeth walked Alexandra to the door. Noah gave them each a quick hug before putting his arm protectively around Alexandra's shoulders. "Lock the door," he instructed.

"We will," Jessica promised.

"And thanks for all your help," Elizabeth added.

"No problem," Noah said, waving goodnight. Alexandra felt his arm tighten around her shoulders as they walked out of the dorm and into the night. "Scared?" he asked.

"Not with you," she responded.

"Really?" he said in pleased voice.

"Yeah. But I have to tell you. I'm really disappointed in you, Noah."

Noah removed his arm and stopped. "Why? What's the matter?"

"You told me you never wound up in dramatic situations, and that none of your friends ever had any major problems. Now here you are, in the thick of everything." A smile hovered around her lips. "I think maybe *you're* the one who thrives on excitement."

Jessica let out a long, unhappy sigh in the dark.

"What's the matter?" Elizabeth asked.

She heard Jessica turn over and punch her pillow several times. "I just can't help thinking."

"About?"

"About Alexandra and Noah. You and Tom. Isabella and Danny. Nina and Bryan. The whole outing tomorrow. Do you realize that Maia and I will be the only two girls without dates?"

"So?"

"So we're both going to look like poor pitiful victims who can't go on with their lives."

Elizabeth sat up and turned on the light. "Lighten up, Jess. First of all, we're going as a big group. And not all the couples are going to be glued at the hip. Tom's going to be on the team bus and then on the field."

"That doesn't count. He doesn't even know about this. It's a surprise for him, remember?"

"OK. Bad example. Winston's going to be driving the Brainmobile, and Denise is going to ride to the game in the minivan with us."

"Yeah. But when we get to the game, they'll be Mr. and Mrs. Braino down on the sidelines."

"Isabella is your best friend, and you know Danny is crazy about you. They're not going to sit there and ignore you."

"That's not the point," Jessica protested, turning over again.

"What *is* the point?"

"The point is that I always attract the wrong kind of guy—and I never realize that he's the wrong kind of guy until it's too late. I'll never have the kind of healthy, normal relationship that all of you do."

"Yes, you will," Elizabeth insisted softly. "You've just got to keep looking. Don't settle for anything less than Mr. Wonderful, and for sure don't settle for Mr. Deranged Homicidal Maniac."

Jessica laughed, and Elizabeth snapped off the light, pushing all the nightmarish, horrible events of the day to the back of her mind. She forced herself to concentrate on the fun that they'd all have tomorrow. *It's going to be a great day—exactly what I need.*

Tom groaned. The producer had said he'd be back in touch before the game, but so far Tom hadn't heard a word. They were down to the wire now, and Tom had fully expected him to call this morning.

Tom groaned again. He'd thought Danny would *never* leave. If Bob had called while Danny was still around, there was no way Tom could have had a candid conversation. Finally, Tom had resorted to feigning nervousness in an effort to discourage conversation and quicken his roommate's departure.

Tom sat down on the bed and chewed anxiously on his fingernails. He wasn't feigning nervousness now. He *was* nervous. But he wasn't sure about what, exactly.

Was it the fact that he was about to play football again—for real? Or was it the fact that he hadn't heard from the producer?

Tom wasn't a pro, but he'd talked to enough people in the news, entertainment, and sports businesses to know that opportunities fell through all the time.

Maybe the whole deal had fallen apart, and Bob just hadn't had the good manners to call and let him know.

Tom glared at the phone. "Ring, why don't you?"

He dropped his head into his hands. If only he knew how to call the guy. But he was in Europe. And Tom hadn't even thought to get his last name when he'd called the first time.

The minutes ticked by, and Tom felt glummer with every passing second. "Getting myself all worked up over this is stupid," he said to the empty room. He stood up, enjoying the feel of his well-exercised and powerful thigh muscles at work. "Story or no story, this has been a great experience." He grabbed his duffle bag and headed toward the door. It was zero hour; he couldn't wait any longer.

Tom was halfway down the hall when he heard the faint ring of the telephone from his room. He dropped his bag and turned so fast that his running shoes made a squeaking sound on the wooden floor. He practically broke the door down as he burst into the room and dove for the phone, knocking several books and a desk lamp to the floor. "Hello? Hello?"

There was a rattle of static and then a voice. "Tom? Tom, it's Bob. I'm calling from Oslo. Can you hear me?"

"I can hear you," Tom shouted.

"How's the story going? Were you able to get on the team? Will you be playing in the game?"

"Yes. I'm on the team, and I was just on my way to the bus. It leaves in five minutes."

"All right!" Bob cried happily through the noise. "I'm having dinner with a network sports exec in about two hours. I'll start the meeting by pitching this story. It sounds great, Tom. Just great."

Tom heaved a big sigh of relief. The guy sounded for real. And the story idea was solid. This thing was going to happen, and it was going to be really great for his career. But he didn't want to go through days of suspenseful waiting again. "Hey, listen, Bob. If I try to get you through VideoNet, who do I ask for? Last time we talked I didn't get your last name."

"It's Hemphill, Tom. Bob Hemphill. But don't worry. I'll call you when I hit the States again. I'm only here for a couple more days."

"I'll be looking forward to it," Tom shouted. "Good-bye. And thanks."

"Good-bye. And be careful." William rattled the piece of newspaper against the receiver one last time for effect. Then he hung up the phone and began to laugh.

"I thought I was going to be late," Danny said when he arrived at the parking lot behind Dickenson. "Where is everybody?"

Isabella, Jessica, and Bryan were the only people there. The three of them were unloading bags of groceries and a cooler from the trunk of Bryan's car.

"They'll be here," Isabella assured him.

Danny looked at his watch. "We don't have that much time." He bent his head back, cupped his hands around his mouth, and began to shout upward in the direction of Elizabeth's window. "Come on, Wakefield. We're not getting any younger. If you don't get out here in thirty seconds, I'm going to bring you out in a fireman's hold."

Jessica began to giggle, but Isabella gave him a dirty look and rolled her eyes. "I can't stand this level of hyperactivity in the morning," she muttered, as she emptied a sack of ice into a cooler chest. "Chill out, Wyatt."

Danny was in too good a mood to get his feelings hurt. He gave Isabella a big, loud kiss on the cheek and then began ripping open the cardboard wrapping around their six-packs of sodas. "I can't help it. I'm psyched about surprising Tom. I just can't believe we have this many people going, and nobody's spilled the beans."

"You're positive Tom doesn't know?" Isabella asked.

"If he does, he's sure a good actor. Before I left the room this morning, he asked me if I knew whether or not anybody was coming." Danny laughed. "I told him I was going to try to catch the last charter bus *if* I got through in the language lab in time."

"Poor Tom," Isabella said. "I hope he hasn't been walking around with his feelings hurt because nobody's made a big deal about the game."

"I think Tom's had enough to think about with this Todd stuff," Jessica said.

"He's got something on his mind, that's for sure," Danny agreed. "Tom's not the most communicative guy in the world, but he's really been closemouthed about rejoining the football team. I just don't know why. And this morning he was like a sphinx."

"I guess he just doesn't want to discuss it," Bryan suggested. "The man made his decision, and that's that."

Danny shrugged. "I guess." A last-minute doubt caused his stomach to sink. "You guys do think we're doing the right thing, don't you? I mean, going up there to surprise Tom? If this *isn't* the right thing to do, then maybe we're doing more harm than good."

Isabella returned Danny's kiss on the cheek and tugged at his earlobe. "We're doing the right thing. And even if we're not, it's too late to change plans now. Here come the troops."

Nina, Denise, Alexandra, Noah, Maia, and Elizabeth all came filing out the back door, laughing and chattering.

"Oops," Jessica whispered to Danny. "I forgot. I've got to take something to Winston. Do you know where he is?"

"In the garage underneath Marsden. I left the minivan in there with the Brainmobile. He's going to drive it over after the team bus leaves. That way we can be sure Tom doesn't spot us leaving campus. If you need to give him something, wait for him here."

"No, I think I'll go on over. It's a sign for the Brainmobile, and I want to be sure it's arranged right. You know how Winston is when he gets rattled."

Winston frantically threw the props into the Braino suitcase and then bore down with all his weight, trying to make the top of the suit-case close.

It was impossible. There was too much stuff inside: giant rubber mallets, rubber chickens, balloons, extra Braino shoes, extra Braino masks, and a Braino football helmet with a tiny mortarboard and tassel glued to the top.

Maybe if he took the helmet out, the suitcase would close. He removed it and threw his body down on top of the hard case. Winston breathed a sigh of relief when he was finally able to click it shut. He examined the oversized helmet.

It was huge, so that it would fit over the Braino mask. Winston slipped it on to make sure he'd still be able to see with it on at the game. Putting on the helmet reminded him that there was supposed to be a Braino football some-where.

He hurried over to the storage locker and rummaged around in the debris that littered the bottom. Shoes, wigs, wacky sunglasses, and mis-cellaneous Braino junk flew in every direction. Unfortunately, there was no football.

Winston was already nervous, but now he was beginning to panic. The comedy bit with the football was a tradition. Mark Janos had given Winston a quick rundown on the basic Braino routines. It had been much more information than Winston could absorb in one session, but Mark had been pretty insistent that the crowd would be unhappy unless Braino kicked the traditional Braino football.

He began racing around the garage, tripping over his shoes and snagging his big Braino pants and shirt on every nail and splinter in the garage.

His anxiety level began to climb, and he could feel himself sweating inside the mask and helmet. It was getting late. He really needed to keep an eye out for the buses and be ready to take the minivan over to Elizabeth's dorm.

Winston jumped up, desperately trying to see if the football was on one of the high shelves that lined the garage. Why couldn't Denise have come with him? She was better at finding things than he was. "I give up," he said angrily, hurrying over to the Brainmobile. He lifted the suitcase and threw it into the backseat.

It landed with a thud, and the top popped open. The contents spilled to the floor. Winston kicked one of the tires in exasperation and removed his helmet, throwing it into the backseat with the rest of the gear. "I'll sort it all when I get—"

He broke off when something heavy smacked him on the back of his head. A sudden burst of white light washed out his entire field of vision. The light began to shrink until there was nothing left but a tiny pinpoint of white in the pitch-black dark.

Winston struggled to remain upright, but it was useless. His arms and legs seemed to have turned to rubber. He tried to say goodnight before his eyes closed and he surrendered to sleep—but he was already on the ground, and his lips wouldn't move.

"Winston? Winston, where are you?" Jessica stood in the Marsden garage and put her hands on her hips. *Where is he?* she wondered irritably.

She saw the Brainmobile and all the props scattered around the backseat. Good grief. Winston was almost as messy as she was. Oh, well, there was no reason to wait for Winston. She could drape the foil sign over the back of the Brainmobile herself.

Jessica reached into her purse to remove the carefully folded sign when a loud crash distracted her. "Winston?"

There was a loud cracking sound, and Jessica's hand involuntarily opened; the sign and her purse dropped to the floor. *I wonder what that noise was?* she thought dreamily, sinking to her knees.

"What's the story?" Bryan called.

Danny jogged back toward the parking lot. "The team bus is gone, and the last couple of charter buses are loading up now." He shook his head. "You can't believe how many Brainos there are."

"Great. Then our guy should be along any minute." Bryan turned toward the girls. Denise, Elizabeth, and Isabella were sitting on the hood of one of the cars, laughing and jeering at Nina and Maia, who were executing a ridiculously lame cheer—deliberately messing up the words and the movements. The culmination of their act was when Nina tried to lift Maia and then sank under the weight.

"I don't even know why we're bothering to go to the game," Bryan commented with a laugh. "They're having enough fun just sitting around the parking lot."

"Attention!" Danny shouted.

The girls ignored him.

"Attention, please. Attention." He clapped

his hands and succeeded, finally, in getting them to look in his direction. "Passengers wishing to use the facilities are advised to do so now," he announced in a booming voice.

Denise jumped down and headed for the door of the dorm. "Don't let them leave without me."

"We're leaving in two minutes whether you're back or not," Elizabeth teased.

"And now," Danny said, spotting the van. "Heeeeeeere's Braino."

Everybody cheered when the purple minivan pulled up. Bryan, Noah, and Danny immediately grabbed the coolers and bags of food while the girls began piling in.

Winston jumped out of the driver's seat and dropped the keys into Danny's palm. "Give Elizabeth a message, will you?" Winston asked in a low, hoarse voice. "Tell her that Jessica changed her mind about going."

"You're kidding! What happened? Where is she?"

Winston shrugged. "I don't know. When she came by the garage, she seemed pretty upset. Then she asked me to bring Elizabeth right back to campus after the game. I'll have the Brainmobile ready to go as soon as the game is over. I can get her back to campus faster than this van can, and that way the rest of you guys don't have to hurry."

"Yeah, OK, sure," Danny answered. "What's the matter with your voice? Are you getting sick?"

"Too much cheering on the quad," Winston said, shifting his weight to the balls of his feet and obviously impatient to be off. "I gotta go. See you there!" He lifted his hand in a farewell wave as he headed back toward Marsden.

"Everybody's going to have to cheer when I come out on the field in my Braino costume and wedding veil," Denise urged.

"We'll be ready," Danny promised.

Elizabeth listened to the laughter and conversation in the van with a smile on her face—but she wasn't really listening.

She stared out the window at the fields and farms that flowed past her view, as the purple minivan cruised up the highway. She couldn't stop wondering about Jessica. And worrying. Jessica had seemed fine that morning, and Elizabeth had felt sure that she was over her gloom from the night before.

Elizabeth cast a glance around the van. True, everybody but Maia had a "date." But on outings like this it didn't matter. And Jessica would have had a blast if she'd come. Everybody was in such a good mood that it would have been impossible for Jessica to feel depressed.

I wish Jess had talked to me about what she was feeling this morning, Elizabeth thought. *I might have been able to change her mind.*

Then she had another thought: Jessica was alone on campus. Most of her friends were at the game. Could she be in any danger?

A sudden wave of panic caused the muscles in her scalp to constrict. "Danny!"

"Yo!"

"Take me back," she urged. "I'm worried about Jessica. I want to go back," she repeated.

"Elizabeth, no!" the entire group chorused.

"I'm worried about Jessica. What if Todd . . ."

"Jessica knows what's going on, and she knows to be careful," Nina said briskly.

"If she gets scared on campus, she can go to the Theta house," Denise added. "There's always a bunch of girls hanging out there. She'll be fine."

Elizabeth sat back in the seat, trying hard to stifle a sense of rising hysteria.

"Denise is right. She'll be fine," Maia insisted quietly. "You've always been there when Jessica needed you, but that doesn't mean you can be her full-time bodyguard. Besides, it's you who's the target, not Jess. The best thing both of you can do is make sure you're not alone. As long as you're with a friend, you'll be fine."

"Besides, think about Tom," Danny added. "What's he going to think if he sees all of us yelling and cheering, and you're not there?"

Elizabeth turned her face toward the window. Her friends were right. Jessica knew how to take care of herself—today was about Tom. She frowned slightly, still unable to get over the feeling there was something he wasn't telling her. Something she should know.

Chapter Fourteen

"Tom, you'll never know how proud of you we are," Mr. Watts said. He put a hand on his son's shoulder, gripped it hard, and gave Tom a playful shake.

Mrs. Watts put her arm around Tom's neck and stood on tiptoe to give her son a kiss on the cheek. "Your father's right."

"I couldn't do it without you guys," Tom said. He grinned at his younger sister. "All of you guys," he added, just in case she didn't know how much he needed her support.

She smiled the pleased, secret smile of a child who's been singled out for attention by her own personal hero.

Tom grabbed his duffle bag and threw it into the trunk. It had been a nice weekend with his folks. Lots of good food and conversation. Most of his old friends had dropped by to see the "football hero." And he'd gotten more compliments and pats on the back than he could count.

He loved coming home. Loved the attention and the admiration. "You guys will be there for the game next weekend, right?" he said to his dad.

"We'll be there," his mother assured him. "Unless your father has an early meeting on Monday morning."

Tom felt his face fall. "You might not be there?"

"We wouldn't miss it," Mr. Watts said, giving Tom's mother a comic but quelling look. "Meeting or no meeting."

"Whew!" Tom joked, wiping imaginary sweat from his brow. "You had me worried there. You guys are my good-luck charms. I depend on your support."

"With all your fans?" his mother teased. "Honestly, how much adulation do you need?" She rolled her yes and lifted her hands in mock exasperation. "My son the egomaniac."

They all laughed, and Tom got behind the wheel of his car. His sister ran to the driver's-side window to have a last, private word with her brother. "We'll be there, Tom. Don't worry. You know Mom. She'll want Daddy to rest all Sunday if he's got an early meeting. But Dad and I can handle her. You can count on us."

Tom leaned out and gave his sister a kiss. "I love you. And if you come, I'll score a touchdown just for you."

She smiled again and jogged beside the window while the car rolled out of the drive.

"Have a good week, sweetheart. And take care." He reached out the window and waved good-bye.

In the rearview mirror, he could see her standing in the middle of the street, waving until his car had turned the corner and was out of sight.

Tom covered his face with his hands. A series of painful pictures and memories raced across his consciousness, threatening to overwhelm him.

His family. Cheering from the stands at his first college game. His baby sister, jumping into his arms as he came striding out of the locker room. "You were way the best one on the team. The best one in the world," she'd shouted.

And then he recalled that horrible day. Two policemen, sympathetic but businesslike, had found him in the locker room. "I'm afraid there's been an accident."

The funeral.

He'd spent days cleaning out the house. Boxing up his parents' clothes and his sister's toys so that they could be passed on to someone

217

living. Someone who could use them. Personal effects were sent to friends and relatives. He'd had the house sold. His father's papers had had to be gone through.

He'd spent agonizing days writing painful thank-you notes to all the people who'd sent flowers, brought food, and pitched in to help him handle the overwhelming amount of work associated with sudden death.

Then there were the long months of grief, self-recrimination, and loneliness. Incredible, indescribable loneliness.

Tom fiercely wiped away a tear that trickled down his cheek. He had to stop it. Had to stop dredging up these memories. He rubbed the heel of his hand over his forehead as if he could somehow erase all the painful images stored in his brain.

He glanced around the bus at the faces of his teammates. Some looked tight-lipped and tense, obviously focused entirely on the competition they were facing. Others looked relaxed. Several laughed and chatted, and quite a few nodded sleepily as the bus rumbled along the highway.

Tom decided the snoozers either had nerves of steel or else had a total lack of respect for curfews. He couldn't imagine napping before a game. He'd never even been able to eat before games.

"Tom, if you don't eat, you won't have the strength to play." His mother pointed to the meat loaf she'd prepared for him. "Just have a bite."

His father and sister laughed and exchanged amused looks. They went through this before every high school game. His mother was always sure he was going to faint on the field from malnutrition.

Tom dropped a kiss on the top of her head. "I'll eat after, I promise. It looks great."

Tom cleared his throat, took a sip from the water bottle he was holding in his hand, and stared determinedly out the window. Up until now, he'd successfully held all those memories at bay. Probably because until this moment, he'd had virtually no time at all for introspection. Since joining the team, he'd done nothing but practice, go to classes, and worry about Elizabeth.

He sighed, wishing she could have been more supportive. It would be nice to have someone at the game rooting him on. But he could hardly expect her to get interested in something like a football game when she was going through such a traumatic experience. And in a million years, he never would have tried to "guilt" her into coming. That was how he killed his family.

Stop! his rational mind ordered. *You did not kill your family, and you know it.* He had to stop feeling sorry for himself. He didn't have any right to wallow in self-pity and possibly jeopardize his ability to play. Being part of a team meant you came through for your teammates.

Everybody on this bus has got problems, he told himself sternly. *None of them are sitting around bawling.*

Yeah, his other little voice countered, *but none of them are orphans, either.*

You're not exactly Little Orphan Annie, Watts. You're a six-foot-one, two-hundred-and-fifteen-pound grown man.

He took some deep breaths and felt his emotions recede. Another few gulps of air and he was back in control. He had a job to do, and he was going to do it well. Still, it would be nice to know there was someone in the stands who was cheering especially for him.

"I don't see him," Nina said.

Maia put on her glasses and turned around in her seat so she could look out the back window. "Me neither."

Denise felt a flicker of worry. Where was

Winston? He should have caught up by now.

"Don't worry. He probably forgot something and went back for it," Noah said.

Maia laughed. "You know how Winston is when he gets rattled." She rolled her eyes. "He gets totally manic."

"I should have ridden with him," Denise said gloomily. This highway went through the mountains; it was a tricky drive. There were hairpin curves, and in some places long stretches where there was no railing. Winston was a pretty wild driver, mostly because he was easily distracted.

"Hey!" Danny admonished. "You know I take everything personally. If I hear one more person say they wish they hadn't come or that they want to go back, I'm going to get my feelings very hurt."

"Ohhhh, poor baby," Isabella soothed. "Don't get your feelings hurt. Everybody's having a great time. Right, folks?"

"Right!"

"Relax, Denise," Alexandra said. "Here he comes."

Denise turned and watched with relief as the Brainmobile came speeding up the highway. She was just about to ask Danny to pull over and let her out to ride with Winston, when Bryan yelled for everybody to duck.

221

"We're passing the charter buses," he shouted. "They're taking a rest stop."

Isabella put her hand on the back of Denise's head and pushed her down.

"Stay down until we're past the team bus," Bryan instructed.

Denise felt the engine in the minivan vibrate as Danny hit the gas and zoomed past the charters.

"OK, everybody up," Danny announced.

Denise sat up and looked out the back window again. Almost a mile back, she could see the brightly painted Brainmobile parked at the rest stop. In the distance, Winston stepped out to perform for the crowd.

"OK! Everybody off."

The door of the team bus opened with a hydraulic whoosh, and row after row of players stood, their tall frames stooping so that their heads didn't bump the roof.

"Ready to rumble?" Pete Gleason asked Tom as he stepped into the aisle and moved toward the door.

"Ready as I'll ever be," Tom answered, stepping into the aisle behind him.

Mo Bentley stood out in the parking lot, counting heads as the team filed off the bus.

"Locker room's to the left. Everybody move, move, move, *move!*"

Leroy Higgins grinned at Tom as they broke into a jog. "Déjà vu all over again," he joked.

Tom laughed. Away games were always like this. The minute the bus arrived, there was a frantic rush to find the locker rooms, get suited up, and go over the plays one last time.

He smelled the unfamiliar air of the State campus and felt a thrill of electric excitement. Lots of players didn't like away games, but Tom did. Being on somebody else's turf meant he had to be a little sharper. A little more alert. It made him think more—and thinking was the key to playing well.

A lot of people thought football was all about brute strength. But it wasn't. It took a lot of brains to play a winning game of football.

Thinking of brains, Tom let out an involuntary chuckle, wondering how Winston Egbert was holding up.

"Winston!" Denise murmured out of the side of her mouth. "What's with you?" She couldn't believe how incredibly inept he was. They'd rehearsed this wedding skit at least four times, and Winston had blown almost every single gag. It was like he had absolutely no idea

223

what they were supposed to be doing.

"Sorry," he rasped.

"Do you, Braino, take this woman to be your lawful wedded wife?" boomed a voice over the PA system. It was a good thing Denise had brought an extra copy of the script and checked with the announcer, because Winston had forgotten to go up to the booth and give him the script.

When she'd arrived, Winston had been busy with the helium tank and balloons, and so flustered and preoccupied that he'd hardly done anything but grunt at her while she pulled on her own Braino costume.

"Braino?" the announcer ad-libbed. "Are you awake down there?"

The crowd in the stands laughed.

Winston still didn't respond, so Denise reached over and honked his big red nose.

The crowd roared.

"Does that mean yes or no?"

Denise honked Winston's nose again.

"How about two honks for yes, one honk for no?"

Denise gave Winston's nose two honks, getting an even bigger laugh from the crowd.

"Are you making this decision of your own free will?"

Denise gave Winston's nose two more honks, and then stood with her hands on her hips, as if daring him to disagree.

The crowd began to applaud, and Denise made the most of it. She gave her bouquet a euphoric sniff before holding it out to a nearby referee to smell. "Don't just stand there," she hissed at Winston, "*do* something!"

When the referee leaned over to smell her flowers, Denise squirted him with water from the bouquet.

The referee laughed good-naturedly, then obligingly pretended to be terrified when Winston grabbed a huge rubber mallet and began chasing him around the field in a jealous rage.

It's about time he did something to make people laugh, Denise thought, watching the ref bob and weave to avoid the mallet.

It was actually pretty funny, as both the referee and Winston got more and more carried away. The referee ran along the sidelines and then vaulted into the stands with Winston hard on his heels.

Denise shook her head in bewilderment. She had no idea what Winston was doing—or where this bit was coming from—but anything was fine with her, as long as it got laughs. She was learning something new about Winston: working from a script wasn't his thing. He must have gotten in front of the audience and just drawn a complete blank. Maybe class clowns were essentially born to improvise.

The referee finally made his escape, and Winston came bounding back over to Denise. He reached into his pocket, produced a large rubber doughnut, and offered it to her with a silent flourish.

Oh well, Denise decided, *if you can't beat 'em, join 'em*. Denise turned up her nose and looked away. She made a show of disdaining the gift.

Winston seemed to catch on to where she was going, because he looked momentarily crestfallen. Then he reached into his other pocket and produced a large rubber diamond ring.

Denise dismissed the offering with a wave of her hand.

Braino teetered around, clutching his chest as if his heart were going to break. After a few moments, he pulled a rubber chicken out of his huge costume.

Now we're cooking, Denise thought. She parodied delight and surprise as she took the rubber chicken. She clutched it to her as if it were something very precious.

"So is the wedding back on?" the announcer asked.

Braino looked at Denise and Denise nodded.

"OK. Then, Braino, with the power vested in me by the NCAA Football Association and the U.S. Bureau of Beef and Poultry Inspectors, I now pronounce you clowns husband and wife. You may kiss the chicken."

Both Denise and Winston pressed their lips against the chicken. They joined hands and ran off the field to wild applause.

"We did it," Denise panted. "We pulled it off. But what happened to all the stuff we rehearsed?"

Winston shrugged. "I just decided to do something different," he whispered.

"What happened to your voice? Are you sick?"

"I think I'm getting a cold," Winston answered. "Better not get too close to me. Tell you what, I'll work the far end of the field, and you stay on this side."

"Yeah. Sure," Denise said, torn between disappointment and worry. She'd never seen Winston like this—so distant. He was almost cold. And he hadn't congratulated her for making their routine work. He hadn't even said anything about forgetting to give the script to the announcer. In fact, he hadn't said *anything* about *anything*. He was acting like a stranger.

227

Maybe she had the wrong take on Winston's feelings. Did he resent her being part of the Braino thing? He wasn't happy about working as a team, she realized with a burst of insight.

Winston was always saying he loved her and wanted to be with her. But the truth of the matter was that deep down, Winston Egbert always had been, and always would be, a solo act.

"Tell *you* what," she said tearfully, pulling off her veil and Braino mask and tossing them at him. "I'll stay far away. I'll stay completely off the field, and you can be Braino all by yourself."

William threw the Braino head and veil on the ground and turned on his heel. He'd had no idea that Denise had been involved in the Braino act. And for the first time since he'd set this drama into motion, he'd come very close to panicking.

He barely knew Winston Egbert—he wasn't in the habit of befriending tall, gangly goofballs. As a result, he had no idea how to impersonate him convincingly with his girlfriend. Everything else relating to the Braino act was no problem. He was athletic, and he'd looked over the props in the garage. Luckily, he'd been to enough games to know the basic Braino moves and traditions. As distasteful as he found pandering to a stadium full of screaming college kids, he hadn't had much choice.

It was fortunate that Denise had gotten angry and stalked off. If she'd insisted on sticking around, it would only have been a matter of time before she detected the deception.

He glanced up into the stands and saw Denise taking her seat—right next to Elizabeth. They were all there, he thought happily, scanning the seats and taking attendance.

Everyone was present and accounted for. Assembled for the last and final act.

Danny Wyatt. Isabella Ricci. Nina Harper. Bryan Nelson. Maia Stillwater. Alexandra Rollins. Noah Pearson. And Denise Waters.

They all sat behind or beside Elizabeth, framing her. William closed his eyes and pictured her sitting alone. The others gone. Blotted out. Then his face broke into a slow and satisfied smile.

"Come on, man. Braino's kicking the football. It's show time!" Mo Bentley slapped Tom on the back and blew on his whistle three times. He let the whistle fall back to his chest and began to shout. "Let's go! Let's go! Let's go!"

Tom found his place in the line and broke into a loose jog as the team filed out of the locker room and onto the field. The announcer called out each player's name and number.

"Number Nineteen, Pete Gleason. Number Twenty-eight, Phil Cooley. Number Eleven, Tom Watts . . ."

There was a loud burst of raucous shouts and applause. Tom heard a familiar voice above all the rest. "Yea, Tom!" He looked up into the stands and felt a blissful sense of joy. Elizabeth stood on her feet, cheering and whistling. Even across a football field, Tom could feel the warmth of her sparkling blue eyes.

And when he saw the rest of his friends around her, he was so stunned he came to an automatic stop. Number Twelve, Leroy Higgins, bumped right into him.

"Hey!" Leroy said in surprise. There were several more startled grunts. "Keep moving, man," Leroy complained. "You just caused a six-player pileup."

Tom laughed. "Sorry about that. I just saw something in the stands that I didn't expect."

"A two-headed elephant?"

"No," Tom replied happily. "A family."

"He's incredible," Noah breathed. "I'd forgotten how good he is."

It was thirteen minutes into the second quarter, and Tom had just scored his fourth touchdown. Elizabeth was so blown away, she could hardly speak. He was a miracle on the field. She'd had no idea he was this good. It was like watching a pro.

"He's Superman," Danny said proudly.

"No way," Bryan argued. "Superman's strong but not too bright. Tom's more like Batman."

"Are you saying Batman is smarter than Superman?" Danny demanded.

"You bet," Bryan answered. "Batman's an intellectual. And way cooler."

"You're nuts," Noah interjected, leaning forward from the seat behind them. "Superman's no slouch in the cerebrum department. Don't forget, he's a journalist."

Nina leaned over to talk to Elizabeth and Maia. "You know, I'll bet when their parents write those big checks every semester, they picture their sons debating Plato's *Republic*."

Alexandra let out a guffaw, and Elizabeth began to laugh. But her eyes never left the field. The line was re-forming.

"Blue-forty-two. *Hike!*" Tom yelled.

The center shot the ball backward into Tom's waiting arms. He caught it, fell back while his teammates got their act together, then started forward toward the goal line.

He had a clear shot, and the SVU fans roared and jumped to their feet as he picked up more and more speed. He was heading for another touchdown.

"Go, Tom!" Elizabeth began to scream. "Go! Go! Go!"

"Come on, Wildman Watts!" Bryan bellowed. Suddenly his eyes got wide. "Look out!"

Two State linebackers who'd been trailing behind Tom suddenly poured on the speed and dove forward. They were rapidly closing the distance between themselves and Tom.

Elizabeth heard the crack of helmets colliding. The three huge players fell to the ground in a pile. Two more State tackles threw their weight on top for good measure.

Three refs ran toward the pile and pulled the State players off of Tom. There was a hush in the stadium as the crowd waited for Tom to rise.

Get up, Elizabeth pleaded mentally. *Please, get up.*

But Tom lay still. A referee signaled to someone on the sidelines, and Mo and Coach Barker ran across the field toward Tom. The players on the bench began to shift uneasily.

"It looks like Tom Watts, Number Eleven, has been injured," the announcer called.

Coach Barker examined Tom, then signaled to someone else. Two players came running out with a stretcher. The four men lifted Tom and placed him on it.

"I've got to get down there," Elizabeth said, choking as they carried him off the field.

"I'll come with you," Maia offered.

"No, stay here," Danny said. He stood up. "I'll go with you, Liz. Come on."

"We'll all go," Alexandra said, standing up.

"Better not," Danny said. "If a whole crowd of us show up, they might not let us into the locker room."

"But how will we know what's going on?" Nina asked, a worried frown on her face.

"I'll go with them and then report back," Noah offered, standing up. He took Elizabeth's arm and helped her rise on shaking legs.

"How is he?" Elizabeth demanded twenty minutes later.

Danny held up his hands. "He's OK. He's conscious, and he's completely lucid. But he's got a huge bump on his forehead and a busted ankle."

Elizabeth started forward. "I want to see him."

Danny put his hand on her shoulder and gently pushed her back. "Wait five minutes,

OK? There are a couple of guys in the shower. They'll freak if they step out and see a girl standing there."

Danny gave Elizabeth his most reassuring smile. "He's fine, Liz. Really. This is football. Tom's used to it."

"He may be," Elizabeth said wryly, "but I'm not."

Danny laughed. "Well, you can give him a piece of your mind in a few minutes, OK? Wait here, and I'll be back to get you."

Elizabeth nodded, and Danny zipped back around the hallway and into the locker room. Tom lay on a table waiting for the doctor.

"Did you tell her I'm fine?" Tom asked immediately.

"Yeah. But you know how it is. She'll believe it when she sees it."

"Thanks for making sure that every friend I've got was here to see me make a fool out of myself."

"Don't thank me," Danny answered with a laugh. "Thank Tim Hemphill."

Tom sat up with a jerk, and Noah snapped his head toward Danny. "Hemphill?" they both said.

Danny frowned in confusion. "Yeah. Tim Hemphill."

Tom raised one eyebrow. "You mean Bob Hemphill?"

"I mean Tim Hemphill. He's on the team. He called me and suggested that I put this whole thing together."

"The only Hemphill I know is a Bob Hemphill. He's not on the team, he's an independent sports producer—and he's in Oslo."

Danny felt a weird, falling sensation in his stomach.

"Tell me about Tim Hemphill," Tom said slowly.

"He called me. Said you'd told him it would mean a lot to you if your friends came to see you play. But who's Bob Hemphill?"

"He called me and suggested I do an undercover piece on postscandal morale. It was his idea for me to take James's place and get back on the team." He shot a look at Noah. "What do *you* know about Hemphill? Tim or Bob?"

"Nothing," Noah answered slowly. "The only Hemphill I know is a Jules Hemphill."

"Who is he? Or who does he say he is?"

"He's exactly who he says he is," Noah answered grimly. "He's a psychiatrist specializing in the treatment of the criminally insane. He works at the Harrington Institution."

Chapter Fifteen

Elizabeth knew something was wrong the second she saw Danny and Noah come striding out of the locker room. "What's going on?" she demanded. "What's wrong?"

"Come on," Danny said curtly, taking Elizabeth's arm and walking her swiftly away from the locker room.

Noah took her other arm, and suddenly Elizabeth's feet seemed to be moving faster than she wanted to go. "Hold it! Hold it!" she cried. "I want to see Tom. Where are we going?"

"You're getting out of here," Danny said. "Now."

"What?" Elizabeth yelled. She dug her heels into the ground, bringing the threesome to a stop. "Would one of you please tell me what's going on?"

"You explain. I'll get Winston." Noah released her arm and ran off, flagging Winston, who was staring at them from a distance.

"Tom wants you to go back to campus," Danny explained to Elizabeth, his eyes darting around the stadium. "Right now. Something's going on. I don't know what, and neither does he. But somebody's been moving us around like chess pieces. And he went to pretty elaborate lengths to get us all here. So our safest move is to leave. You most of all."

"I don't understand," Elizabeth said. "This is crazy."

"You're right." Danny nodded. "It is crazy. But since we don't know what we're dealing with, let's all do what Tom says and get away from here."

Elizabeth watched as Noah explained the situation to Winston. Winston gave a couple of brisk nods, and followed Noah back over to where they stood.

"Just leave the Braino stuff," Danny said to Winston before he had a chance to speak. "Tom'll get somebody from the team to bring it back on the bus. You just get Elizabeth out of here now. We'll get the others and be right behind you."

"What about Tom?" Elizabeth cried as Winston

took her arm in a surprisingly painful grasp.

"He'll ride back with the team," Danny answered. "The doctor is taping his ankle now, but he doesn't want us to wait."

"Will he be safe?"

Danny's grim face cracked in a smile. "He's surrounded by about six tons of manpower. The entire SVU football team. Yeah. I'd say he's about as safe as a man can be."

"Come on," Winston said hoarsely. "Let's get started. The second act is just about to start."

"You mean the second half," Elizabeth responded automatically.

"No," Winston replied. "I mean the second act—complete with a surprise second-act character."

If that was a joke, Elizabeth didn't get it. But before she could ask for an explanation, Winston was walking toward the parking lot, dragging her along with him.

"I still can't get over it," Elizabeth said ten minutes later. They were on the road and speeding back toward campus. "I mean, I guess on one level I knew Tom was this great athlete, but it wasn't real until I saw him with my own eyes. He was incredible, wasn't he?"

Winston said nothing.

"Winston?" Elizabeth prompted. "Are you listening to me? Didn't you think Tom was incredible?"

When Winston turned to face her, his eyes glittered strangely behind the Braino mask. "Winston? Are you going to take off that mask?"

"No," he replied shortly.

Elizabeth sighed and settled back in her seat. It wasn't like Winston to be so surly and uncommunicative. But he was probably scared. And she doubted he was thrilled about having to leave in the middle of his Braino debut. She also knew he'd had a fight with Denise.

Elizabeth wondered what the fight had been about. Denise hadn't gone into any detail— she'd just sat beside Elizabeth in depressed silence until Tom's accident.

Elizabeth decided not to ask Winston anything about it. And she wouldn't ask him about his Braino act, either. It was probably less emotionally threatening to focus on topics that didn't have anything to do with him, his act, Denise, or the bizarre events that were taking place. That was fine—Elizabeth didn't want to have to think too much about any of those things, either.

She decided to concentrate on Tom instead.

"You know what I love the most about Tom?" she began.

Winston let out something that sounded like a rude snort.

"Pardon me?" she said, before she noticed that the eighteen-wheeler in front of them had abruptly slowed and showed no signs of turning off the road.

Winston flipped on the blinker and focused his attention on the truck, as he accelerated past it on a strip of road with a double yellow line down the center.

"Relax," she begged. "We'll get there."

Winston said nothing and completed the pass.

"Going back to Tom," she began again. "He's just such an incredibly remarkable guy. An intellectual. An athlete. A journalist. He's . . ."

"Tom Watts is a loser," Winston announced.

"What?"

"Tom Watts is a clumsy oaf!" he shouted, banging his fist on the steering wheel. "Why did he have to be a hero? Why did he have to show off? He shouldn't have gone for that touchdown!"

Elizabeth wondered if Winston had been drinking. In the years she'd known him, he'd never acted this way before.

Winston's body shook as he struggled to control his temper. She watched his knuckles

241

turn white as he gripped the steering wheel. "You'll have to forget Tom Watts," he snapped.

"Forget Tom?"

"I don't want to hear another word about Tom Watts. He's completely ruined everything. Everything! He was supposed to ride back in the van and die with the rest of your hangers-on."

"*Die?* What are you talking about?" Elizabeth stuttered. "Winston. What's the matter with you? What are you talking about? Are you insane?"

"Don't you *ever* call me insane!" he screamed, sending flecks of saliva in every direction. He violently jerked the wheel, passing a sedan with a squeal of his tires and only inches to spare.

The driver of the sedan honked loudly, but the Brainmobile never slowed. It kept accelerating, as if it were keeping pace with the driver's escalating rage. "Maybe it's better this way," he seethed. "It's better that he live and know that when it comes to love, he's a loser."

Elizabeth felt her body turning icy cold. Winston Egbert wasn't under the mask and makeup.

"Tom Watts is a chimp. An amoeba. A single-celled molecule masquerading as a human being."

There was something about the tone. The lift of the chin. The toss of the head. His voice and manner were familiar. The hauteur. She'd seen it before.

But only in her worst nightmares had she expected to see it again.

It couldn't be. It simply couldn't be true. It had to be someone else. "Todd?" she gasped in a shaking, tentative voice.

There was another rude snort from behind the mask. "Todd? I think not."

Elizabeth's pupils began to dilate, and she felt the earth shift like the deck of a ship caught in a violent, unstoppable storm.

"Todd's here?" Maia said in a voice of bewilderment. "How do you know he's here? Did somebody see him?"

"Todd?" Alexandra exclaimed. "What's he doing here? I don't understand. And where's Elizabeth?"

"If everybody will please get into the van, I'll try to explain. But we need to get going. OK?" Danny took Maia's arm and helped her into the van. He was trying very hard to stay cool, calm, and collected, but it wasn't easy. Not only was he freaked out—he felt guilty. He was the one who'd orchestrated this whole thing. He'd played right into some lunatic's hands.

There hadn't been time to fill everyone in. The whole group chattered and fretted in the vast parking lot as they milled around the van, deciding who was going to sit where.

Danny clenched his teeth, trying not to lose patience with them for moving so slowly. It wasn't their fault, he reminded himself. They didn't know what was going on. All they knew was that one minute they were sitting in the stands enjoying a football game, and the next minute Danny and Noah were rousting them out of their seats and hustling them toward the van like a SWAT team making an arrest.

"I sat in the back driving up," Nina balked as Danny tried to boost her into one of the back-seats. "I want to sit in the front seat this time. I get carsick in the back."

"Me too," Bryan said.

"I'll switch with you," Isabella offered.

"Would you guys just get in the van so we can get out of here?" Danny finally yelled, stamping his foot on the pavement.

There was a stunned silence.

"I'm sorry," Danny said immediately. "I'm sorry. There's just a lot of weird stuff going on, and the sooner we get out of here, the safer we'll all be."

"Should we call the police or something?" Denise asked.

Danny shook his head. "I think we need to get back to campus as soon as possible. We'll call the police there. They've got the background on Todd."

"So you believe Todd's behind this?" Noah asked.

"I don't think there's any question about it," Danny answered. "Do you? I don't know how or why he knew about Dr. Hemphill and decided to use his name, but there's obviously a lot about this we don't understand."

"Who's Dr. Hemphill?" Nina, Bryan, and Maia all asked in unison.

Danny opened his mouth to explain, but before he could answer, there was a muffled clunking from underneath the van.

"What was that?" Isabella asked.

Danny frowned. "I don't know." He climbed out and peered under the van. There was nothing beneath it but an expanse of oil-stained concrete.

A second thump actually caused the van to rock slightly.

"What *is* that?" Denise asked, rolling down her window and sticking her head out.

Danny shrugged. "I don't know."

Suddenly, they heard a series of bangs and a muffled cry.

"My gosh!" Danny gasped. "It's coming from the luggage compartment." He reached down and pulled the handle of the trunk space.

Danny jumped backward as a Braino clown came rolling out with his hands tied together and a piece of tape over his mouth.

Denise let out a little shriek, and her hands flew to her mouth. She exploded out the door. "Winston!"

"Winston?" the entire group chorused.

Denise was on her knees beside Winston before Danny could even squat down. Her fingers reached down and ripped the tape from Winston's mouth.

"Ouch!" he yelled.

"Sorry," Denise said.

Winston sat up, lifted his bound hands, and pulled off the Braino mask. "Wow! I don't think I ever want to wear that thing again. I felt like the man in the iron mask."

"What happened?" Danny demanded, pulling the ropes from around Winston's hands. "Was Todd here in the parking lot? Did you see him? Did Elizabeth get away? Where's the Brainmobile?"

"To answer your questions: I don't know. I

246

don't know. I don't know. And . . . I don't know." Winston lifted his hand and felt the back of his head. His hair was matted with blood. "The last thing I remember, I was in the garage at Marsden. The next thing I know, I'm waking up inside a dark compartment listening to you guys argue about who's sitting in the front and who's sitting in the back."

Danny felt like shaking Winston. Didn't he have any idea how serious this was?

"You mean, you've been in there since before the game? It wasn't you who drove the Brainmobile to the game? And it wasn't you who married me on the field?" Denise cried in a thrilled voice.

"Well, you don't have to sound so happy about it," Winston complained.

Danny met Noah's gaze. His large dark eyes held as much worry and panic as Danny's. "So if Winston's been in here since before the game . . ." Danny said.

". . . who's driving Elizabeth?" Noah finished.

"Get everybody inside and buckled up, will you?" Danny cried, taking off across the parking lot at a run.

"Where are you going?" Denise cried.

"To get Tom," Danny shouted back over his

shoulder. "Busted ankle or no busted ankle, he'll bust our chops if we don't tell him what's going on."

"Can anybody hear me?" Jessica shouted in desperation. "If anybody can hear me, please let me out. I'm locked in."

Jessica's head ached so badly, she could hardly stand up in the . . . She groped around. The *what*? Where was she? In a closet?

Her hands felt walls on four sides but couldn't find a doorknob or a handle. "Let me out!" she screamed as loudly as she could.

The noise of her own voice made her head hurt even worse. She gingerly felt the base of her skull and winced. It felt damp. Was she bleeding?

Jessica tried to remember where she'd been before she had blacked out. But everything beyond being in the parking lot behind Dickenson Hall was a fog.

"How did I get here?" she whimpered. "And where is everybody? Where's Elizabeth?" Suddenly, the events of the last few days came flooding back, practically knocking her to her feet again. Todd. The dolls. The attempted murder of Celine.

Who had put her in this dark place?

Her heart pounded as she began to bang on the door in panic. "Please!" she yelled. "Someone help me!"

There was a clang and a scuffling sound on the other side of the wall. Jessica immediately stopped her shouting and banging.

She heard footsteps coming toward her, and her heart gave a sickening thump.

Maybe advertising the fact that she was alive and well had been a very stupid thing to do. She shrank back against the wall and sank down, trying to make herself as small as possible.

On the other side of the wall, she could hear someone fumbling with a handle. Whoever it was rattled the entire structure as he tried to force the door open—then there was the sound of a blow being struck.

Jessica shrank back. Had someone come to her rescue? Or had someone come to finish off the job they'd started earlier?

A third, savage blow caused the door to pop open, and Jessica saw a crack of light. She waited in heart-stopping agony for someone to wrench the door open and force her out of the closet.

She waited. And waited. Finally, she heard calm, unhurried footsteps walking away.

Obviously, her rescuer meant no harm.

Jessica opened the door, stepped out, and realized she was still in the Marsden garage. "Hello?" she called out, peering around to see who was there.

No one answered.

There was a loud creak, which Jessica recognized as the sound of a heavy exit door. She hurried around a line of parked cars and saw the door that led to the dorm swing shut with a loud and reverberating bang.

Jessica ran to the door, opened it, and looked up the concrete stairs just in time to see a tall, slim male disappear through a door that led to the dorm. "Hey!" she shouted. "Wait! Come back so I can thank you!"

But the guy gave no sign that he'd heard.

"How weird!" she muttered. The pain in her head was excruciating. There was no way she could go to the game now.

Game!

Jessica looked quickly around. The Brainmobile was gone, and so was the van. Had they left without her?

Then she looked at her watch and gasped. "Jeez!" This was unbelievable. She had been unconscious for almost four hours. Jessica began to run. What had happened? Where was everybody? And how could they have gone off and left her like this? The most terrifying question of all made her come to an abrupt halt. Where was Elizabeth?

"I think we'll go to Switzerland first. I have several numbered accounts, and I doubt that anyone will look for us there." He laughed. "I doubt that anyone will look for *me*, at any rate. After all, I'm dead already. You're the only person in the world who knows I'm alive. You and Celine."

Celine? What was he talking about? The road skimmed by, and Elizabeth's breath caught in her throat as the Brainmobile skidded around a hairpin mountain curve.

"They'll look for you, though," William continued in a voice of deep satisfaction. "They'll lock Todd Wilkins up for your murder, and he'll spend the rest of his squalid, pathetic life maintaining his innocence while they look for your body."

He reached over and patted her arm. "And all the time you'll be with me. I'll treat you well, Elizabeth. Like a princess. You deserve to be treated like royalty."

"Is that why you've spent the last several weeks terrorizing me?" she couldn't help asking, sure now that it had been William, not Todd.

The car careened from one lane to the other with a squeal of tires as William succumbed to another spasm of uncontrollable fury. "I did it for you! Can't you see that?" He took another corner too fast and fought the wheel for control as they went into a slight skid.

Elizabeth closed her eyes and gripped her hands more tightly to keep her body from shaking.

William seemed to regain control of himself as he regained control of the car. "I had to make you think Todd was mad. I had to make everyone think he was mad. I had to make them believe that he would kill you. And kill Celine." He snapped his fingers. "Remind me, we need to do something about her before we leave. We can't afford to leave her alive."

Elizabeth sat rigid with fear, her hands squeezed tightly together in her lap. He was insane. Completely and absolutely insane. *Remind me, we need to do something about Celine.* He might have been talking about stopping the newspaper or picking up his cleaning before a ski trip.

"So it was you who tried to kill Celine?" she whispered as they neared a second curve in the road.

"Of course," he answered in a pleased, condescending voice.

On one side of the road, there was a sheer drop of several hundred feet. On the other side, a soaring cliff wall jutted upward.

William's lip lifted in a sneer. "You don't think that Todd would actually have the fortitude or the guts to commit murder, do you? Or suicide. He's not like us. We'll live life on our own terms—or we won't live it at all. Isn't that right?"

Elizabeth swallowed hard, fighting the impulse to begin screaming hysterically. He was mad, and he was dangerous, but cooperating with him was only a temporary solution. She had no doubt whatsoever that no matter what she said, and no matter what she did, he would kill her before the end of this day.

She watched the road carefully, trying to remember where the curves were. She cast her mind back—yes, there was the tree with the split trunk. If she recalled correctly, she had noticed that trunk right after they'd turned a particularly sharp corner. Denise had complained that Danny was driving too fast.

The road began to bend. Elizabeth took a deep breath, reached over, and grabbed the hair on the side of William's Braino mask. She gave it a savage yank, twisting it so that it sat sideways on his head.

A distorted and misshapen Braino face stared at her from the side of William's head. "I can't see!" William shrieked. He took his hands from the wheel to remove the mask, and as he did, Elizabeth grabbed the wheel and turned it as far to the right as she could.

His foot pounded the brake, but it was too late. Her own foot had already hit the gas pedal and rammed it against the floor. The car went into a spin, making a sound like a thousand fingernails on a blackboard.

Elizabeth felt strangely calm, watching the scenery pass by and counting the revolutions of the vehicle. One. Two. Three. They were turning in slow motion, and Elizabeth saw the birds in the trees, the colors of the rocks, and the billowing clouds. It was almost peaceful.

There was a screaming sound far in the distance. High and shrill. It took her a long time to realize it was William. "Are you insane?" she heard him scream.

The car hurtled toward the cliff wall and collided with a thundering crash of grinding metal and splintering glass.

Elizabeth felt the grip and bite of her seat belt as it jerked her back against her seat. Out of the corner of her eye, she saw William lurch forward, bounce off the windshield, and then slump over the wheel.

The noise from the collision seemed to echo on and on forever, reverberating throughout the canyon. Elizabeth covered her ears until the din subsided.

At last, it was over. All was quiet, and William White lay slumped over the wheel, the Braino head still twisted sideways on his head.

Elizabeth reached out with a curious, detached floating feeling and pulled off the mask. She placed her hand under William's chin and gently turned his face toward hers.

He stared at her with blank, unseeing eyes. "Don't ever call me insane," she said quietly.

Chapter
Sixteen

The passenger door wrenched open and a hand reached inside the car and clutched her arm. "Elizabeth! Elizabeth, are you OK?"

A racking sob shook her shoulders, and she felt the hand grip harder. "Elizabeth. Say something. Come on. Speak to me. Tell me you're OK."

The voice was gentle but firm. It was a voice that was full of concern, compassion, and common sense. A voice she'd heard almost all of her life. "Todd!" she cried, leaning sideways and falling into his arms.

"It's OK," he whispered, holding her tightly. "It's OK."

"I'm so sorry," she said, still weeping. "I'm so sorry about everything. I'm sorry I thought it was you. I'm sorry . . ."

"It's *all right*," Todd insisted, grimacing at the sight of William's body. "It's over now. It's all over. Let's see if you can stand up."

"What are you doing here?" she asked, as he helped her from the car.

"I followed you guys to the game and sat behind you in the stands. When you went down to the locker rooms, I followed. And when you left the stadium, I stayed on your tail."

She lifted her head and looked curiously at the black Jeep Cherokee parked by the side of the road. "Where did you get that car?"

Todd pulled off his Braino mask, wiped his forehead, and gave her a sheepish grin. "I stole it."

"Faster," Tom urged.

"I can't go any faster and keep this van under control," Danny said tightly. He pumped the brakes, slowing the van down on a slope so that he could press the gas when they took the curve. When he tapped the brake, he heard a strange sound.

"There they are!" Maia shouted, breaking the tense silence.

Tom leaned forward. "Pull up behind the Brainmobile," he instructed as the wrecked car came into view.

Elizabeth stood by the side of the road, waving her arms.

Danny guided the van onto the shoulder of the road and pressed the brake pedal. There was a snapping sound but no response from the van. Danny stomped his foot down on the brake as hard as he could, but the vehicle didn't even slow.

Beside him, he heard Isabella scream as the van plowed into the wrecked Brainmobile, sending it sliding across the road and over the edge of the cliff.

"What the . . ." Todd automatically shielded Elizabeth as an explosion came roaring up out of the canyon.

"William wasn't just ranting and raving," Elizabeth gasped. "He said they were all going to die."

"What?"

"He said they were all going to die," Elizabeth repeated in an agonized voice. "He must have done something to the van. That's why they couldn't stop."

Todd grabbed her arm and began running toward the Jeep. "He must have cut the brake lines."

"Nobody can drive this road with no

brakes," Elizabeth whispered as Todd helped her into the Jeep. "It's certain death."

Todd started the engine and threw the Jeep into gear, spinning the tires and sending gravel in all directions as they lurched out onto the road. "I think that's exactly what William was counting on."

Inside the van, no one said a word. Every single passenger held their breath, painfully aware of the danger they were facing.

Alexandra felt Noah take her hand. She stared at him with stricken eyes. "I'm sorry." She whispered the words so softly that they were hardly more than the movement of her lips.

"What for?" he mouthed back.

She shook her head, unable to speak, and dropped her eyes to her lap. Because of her, Noah was going to die. If it hadn't been for her, Noah would never have gotten involved in all this mess.

A tear trickled down her cheek. Noah said nothing, but she felt his finger touch her cheek, brushing away the tear.

Denise held on to Winston's hand for dear life. She lifted her eyes and studied his profile. Winston was goofy, silly, and alarmist. But now, in a real crisis, he seemed completely self-possessed. For the first time in their entire relationship, he looked completely serious. He seemed to sense that she was watching him and turned toward her. "We'll be OK," he whispered into her ear.

"No, we won't," Denise said, choking and leaning into his arm.

He put his free arm around her and squeezed. "Yes, we will. Because I love you."

Denise swallowed hard. "I love you, too," she whispered back.

"Are you serious?"

"We're about to die. Would I joke around at a time like this?"

Tom's stomach felt like a clenched fist. Fury, fear, and a sense of responsibility for his friends churned in his gut like a cement mixer.

What he really wanted to do was leap from the van, backtrack until he caught up with Todd, and then strangle the life out of him.

But a busted ankle was going to make that plan hard to carry out. Besides, he could never abandon this many people in danger.

"Why are we picking up speed?" he asked Danny in a low voice, so that the others wouldn't hear.

261

"We're headed down the mountain," Danny murmured. "And this road turns about every half mile."

"What are our options?"

"We don't have any," Danny said simply.

Elizabeth watched in horror as the purple minivan ahead of them took the hairpin curve at top speed.

Todd hit the gas, and the Jeep began speeding forward.

"What are you doing?"

Todd pointed up the mountain. "There's a very fancy ranch hidden up there. It belongs to an SVU alum. The family who owns it had a party for the basketball team there at the beginning of the year."

"And?"

"And there's a private road that leads to the house. You get on it by turning off the highway. It's about two miles ahead."

Elizabeth shook her head. "What are you saying?"

"I'm saying I have a plan."

"A good plan?"

"No. But right now it's the only plan we've got."

*   *   *

Danny glanced over at Isabella. She sat with her back as straight as a rod, staring ahead at the road with large, unblinking eyes.

She was beautiful. The most beautiful girl he'd ever dated. And she was beautiful inside, too. Had he ever told her how achingly beautiful she was? *If we get out of this alive,* he vowed, *I'm going to tell her every day. Every hour. Every . . .*

"Watch it," Tom cautioned. "We're coming up on another curve."

Danny gripped the wheel with both hands and forced himself to watch the road instead of Isabella's beautiful face.

"Watch out!" Bryan shouted as the van swerved into the other lane and barely missed an oncoming VW. The VW let out a series of indignant beeps.

"Better ride the horn so they can hear us coming around the turns," Tom instructed.

Isabella turned toward Danny and gave him a brave and tremulous smile. "That's what they do in Europe." Her voice shook, but she was trying hard to keep her tone light. "I'm just pretending we're late to a party in the South of France."

"I'm just pretending I'm not here," Winston said from the back.

There were a few snorts of laughter from the otherwise tense and silent group.

Then, suddenly, Denise let out a surprised cry. "Move over," she shouted. "They're passing us."

"Who?" Danny yelled.

"Elizabeth and Todd!"

"What!" Tom jerked his head around, but Danny kept his eyes glued to the road, fighting hard to control the wheel.

"I don't believe this," Bryan breathed. "What's he doing? Trying to race us?"

Danny cut his eyes to the left and saw the Jeep pulling up parallel to the van. Elizabeth and Todd both waved their arms.

"What is she saying?" Nina cried. "She's shouting something."

"Don't let them pass," Tom said curtly. "Whatever Todd's up to, we're better off with him behind us instead of in front where he can cut us off."

Danny hit the gas, pulled out ahead of the Jeep, and straddled the center of the road.

"Follow us!" Elizabeth shouted, trying desperately to make herself heard over the horn. "Let us pass!"

Todd wove back and forth, trying to pass on

264

the right and then on the left. But the purple van stubbornly rode the line, making it impossible to pass on either side.

Elizabeth took off her seat belt.

"What are you doing?" Todd shouted.

"Take your hands off the wheel and hold them up," she shouted.

"Are you nuts?"

"They don't trust you. They probably think you're holding a gun on me." She began to stand on the seat and then tumbled back to a sitting position as the Jeep hit a pothole.

"Sit down," he yelled. "You're going to get killed."

"We're all going to get killed if they don't get out of the center of the road," she shouted.

"That is one very sick boy," Bryan breathed.

"Bryan! Shhh," Nina fussed.

"Look for yourself!" he insisted.

Everyone in the van turned, and Tom's heart stopped. Elizabeth stood in the passenger seat of the open Jeep, waving her arms, and Todd had his hands raised in the air, steering with his knees.

"Stay cool," Danny said to Tom. "He's just trying to freak us out."

"Maybe they're trying to tell us something,"

Winston suggested. "Look at Elizabeth. She's shouting."

"Lay off the horn," Tom said.

Danny removed his hand, and Tom leaned over and unrolled the window.

". . . LOW . . . US . . ." He heard Elizabeth's faint voice over the roar of the van's engine. She gestured broadly, pointing to the van, and then to the Jeep.

"What did she say?" Nina asked.

"She's telling us to follow them," Winston said. He turned to Denise. "I didn't spend two weeks in mime school for nothing."

"Think it's a trick?" Danny asked Tom.

Tom felt his stomach muscles clench again. He had no idea what Todd was trying to pull. But right now they had two choices—trust Todd Wilkins or die.

"Let 'em pass," he said.

"It worked!" Elizabeth cried, sitting down in her seat as the purple van hugged the right side of the road.

The Jeep zoomed forward, and as it passed the van, Elizabeth saw Tom's pale, solemn face staring intently at hers. She blew him a kiss and then gestured again for the van to follow.

"Hold on," Todd warned. "And make sure

266

you're buckled up. We're about to hit a mother of a curve, and I can't slow down or they'll rear-end us."

Elizabeth grabbed her seat belt and snapped it efficiently into place.

"Here we go," Todd muttered. "If we don't make it, Liz, you've been a great friend."

"No, I haven't. But if we do make it, I promise to be a better one."

The road turned, and Todd pressed the gas as he pulled the wheel around. Elizabeth gripped the edge of her seat and felt her nails dig into the upholstery. The Jeep swung around the curve on two wheels.

Elizabeth held her breath, listening to the squeal of the tires and waiting for the flip. The turn seemed to go on and on forever, until she finally heard the reassuring thump of the other two wheels touching back down on the road. "Nicely done," she muttered to Todd.

Todd threw her a crooked smile. Elizabeth twisted around in her seat, holding her breath. They had made it in one piece, but would the van?

Danny gripped the wheel and felt a strange sense of calm descend upon him as the van took the curve. It was beyond his control now.

What was meant to be was meant to be.

Everybody inside the van lost it, and Danny could almost imagine that he was on a roller coaster surrounded by screaming passengers.

He felt the centrifugal force push him back against his seat and then release as the van safely rounded the curve. He couldn't help letting out a whoop of surprised glee. They were still on the road, and they were still alive. If this weren't such a nightmare, it would be fun. Sort of.

He tightened his fingers around the wheel again and wiped the sweat off his brow with the shoulder of his T-shirt. Everyone inside the van applauded wildly.

Todd eyed the thick foliage along the road until his eye found what he was searching for. "Here's the drive. Hang on and hope they figure out what we're doing."

He turned sharply to the right. In the rearview mirror, he saw the expanse of sky that soared above the canyon that was now directly behind them.

The Jeep slowly began losing speed as it climbed the steep private road. He checked the rearview mirror again and saw the van pull in behind him.

Todd felt the engine balk. The wheels were

having to work harder, and he hit the gas. They couldn't stop, and the van behind them couldn't afford to start rolling backward—not yet.

Danny felt the van immediately begin to slow as the vehicle moved uphill. "OK," he said to Tom. "I see what we're doing. Do you?"

Tom nodded. "Unlock the doors and take off your seat belts," he instructed the others.

"What are we doing?" Noah asked.

"Getting ready to jump," Danny explained.

"We're going to jump from a speeding van?" Maia repeated in a shocked voice. "I don't think I can do that."

"Look behind you," Tom instructed.

Danny peered in the rearview mirror to see what Tom was showing Maia. "At some point we're going to lose most of our speed," Tom explained in a very conversational tone. "And then this van is going to start rolling backward. When it does, it's going to roll right across the highway and over the cliff that's directly behind us. So what we'd like to do is make sure everybody's out by the time the van starts rolling backward." He smiled at Maia. "Still think you can't do it?"

Maia swallowed hard and unbuckled her seat belt.

"Good girl," Tom said approvingly.

Danny actually had to pump the gas pedal to keep the van moving now. "Get ready," he instructed in a terse tone. "Open all the doors."

Winston, Bryan, and Isabella all opened the doors in the back. Isabella leaned across Danny, opened his door, and kissed his cheek before returning to her seat.

"I want everybody to stay calm," Tom announced. "And we're going to do this in order. Bryan, Nina, Denise—you guys jump from the left door. Maia and Isabella, you jump from the right. Then Alexandra, Noah, and Winston. I'll be behind you. Jump and roll clear of the van as fast as you can. *Don't* wait to see if the person ahead of you is out of the way. Just go ahead and jump. If you wait, you're jeopardizing your own life and the life of the person behind you. Everybody clear?"

"I hope so man, because this is it," Danny said. "We're running out of steam."

"Maia, here you go," Tom said.

Maia screamed as Tom grabbed her by the arm and lifted her out of her seat. He thrust her out the open door. Danny couldn't help feeling a lump of pride in his throat when it was Isabella's turn. Isabella lost no time at all and needed no assistance. "I love you," he heard her say. The next thing he knew, she was gone.

"Did she make it?" he yelled at Tom. "Did she make it?"

But Tom was too busy yelling to answer. "Go, Alexandra! Now. Noah, this is it! Great. Come on, Winston." His directions were firm and controlled; only the slight tremor in his voice gave away his fear.

The van was rolling backward now, picking up speed. Danny fought hard to keep it from flipping. He could hear people yelling and had a vague peripheral view of bodies strewn along the road.

"Everybody's out," he heard Tom say. "It's you and me, pal."

Danny gripped the wheel, staring in the rearview mirror. The edge of the highway was rushing toward them. "Let's go," Tom urged.

Danny tried to open his hands but couldn't. It was as if they had been locked into position so long he couldn't unclench them.

"Let's go!" Tom shouted.

"I can't," Danny said through gritted teeth.

"What do you mean, you can't? Let go, Danny. Let go."

"You go," Danny ordered. "Jump. Jump now!" he screamed.

Tom looked at him with his mouth agape.

Danny stared at the rearview mirror, watching oblivion looming up behind him.

Out of the corner of his eye, he saw Tom lunge toward him and then . . . nothing.

Elizabeth ran down the road as the van hurtled backward. "Tom!" she screamed. "Tom, get out! Tom!"

She saw Isabella stumble to her feet and shake her head to clear it after her fall. "Danny?" she called out, lifting her large eyes and searching the road.

The van was practically at the bottom of the road.

"Tom!" Elizabeth shrieked.

The van began skidding across the highway. Elizabeth and Isabella both let out bloodcurdling screams when it reached the lip of the cliff.

Suddenly, two bodies fell out the passenger side onto the highway. Less than a second later, the van tipped over the side of the cliff and disappeared.

Tom lay on the concrete, stunned, with Danny in his arms. He'd never in a million years thought he'd punch Danny Wyatt. But he had. Caught him in the jaw and knocked him out cold. He'd have to remember to apologize, he thought idly.

He took a few deep breaths, feeling suddenly sleepy. He fought the feeling, recognizing it as a concussion symptom. Still, he couldn't help closing his eyes. His lids felt so heavy. Surely closing them for five seconds wouldn't hurt.

Chapter
Seventeen

"What time is it?" Tom demanded.

A soft hand closed around his. "Tuesday," he heard Elizabeth answer.

"Tuesday?" He struggled to sit up, but the pain in his head forced him back down.

"That's better," Elizabeth said approvingly.

He looked around. He was in a hospital room. In a bed. Suddenly, he remembered their nightmarish ride. "How is everybody? How's Danny? What happened?"

"You mean what happened since you dove out of a speeding van and hit the concrete head-first—and had two concussions in one day? Or what happened over the last few weeks that started this whole thing?"

"Start with what happened since I hit the concrete headfirst."

Elizabeth blew out her breath. "Well, to start with, everybody survived the jump. All of us, including you, have been in the newspapers and news constantly. Noah and Alexandra are fine, and Noah says this is the most exciting thing that's ever happened to him. And as horrible as it was at the time, he's really happy, because now he'll have something to talk about at parties for the rest of his life."

Tom laughed.

"Winston and Denise both turned in their Braino resignations. They decided clown work is just too dangerous. Danny is fine, except that he suspects you socked him in the jaw—or else that he hit his face in the fall. The doctors weren't able to determine what happened, and he can't remember much of what happened after people started to jump."

"I did hit him in the jaw," Tom admitted. "But let's not tell him."

Elizabeth smiled and sat down at the edge of his bed. "It'll be our secret." She settled herself more comfortably and squeezed his hand a little tighter. Tom decided he'd never seen her look more beautiful. "Maia, Bryan, and Nina are fine, but all of them fell into a patch of poison ivy and they're covered with a really unattractive pink goo."

Tom chuckled. "Ouch! Don't make me laugh. It makes my head hurt."

Elizabeth smiled. "Sorry. I'm just so happy you're OK."

"Am I OK?"

Elizabeth nodded. "Yeah. You are. All your tests look fine. But you did get conked on the head twice, so they've kept a pretty close eye on you for the last couple of days."

"What about you?" Tom asked, taking her hand.

"I've been keeping a pretty close eye on you, too."

Tom's face turned serious. "What I meant was—who's been keeping an eye on *you*?"

"Todd."

"Todd?"

Elizabeth nodded. "It's a long story, Tom. But William White was behind all of it."

"I guess you'd better tell me everything."

Twenty minutes later, when the nurse came in with some soup and Jell-O for Tom, he lay back on his pillows staring at the ceiling in shock. "It's unbelievable," he breathed. "Absolutely unbelievable."

Elizabeth shook her head. "Unbelievable doesn't even begin to cover it. It's so unbelievable that I don't think anything in my whole life could ever surprise me again."

Tom reached for the Jell-O and took a bite of the wobbling red gelatin.

"Forget I said that," Elizabeth said, laughing. "I take it back. I'm surprised to see you eat that stuff. I never pegged you as a Jell-O man."

"See what you find out about people when you share a near-death experience?" he said, lifting his brows and taking another bite. "I love Jell-O."

They both laughed. "I haven't even told you who's recovering nicely in a room right down the hall," Elizabeth said.

"Tell me. I'm not exactly in the mood for surprises."

"The one and only Celine Boudreaux."

"Really? That's good . . . I think."

Elizabeth giggled. "Even Celine doesn't deserve the wrath of William, although I guess it's taken pretty drastic measures for her to realize that."

Their conversation broke off when the door swung open and an older man wearing a dark-gray suit and carrying a briefcase stepped politely into the room. "Excuse me. I'm sorry to intrude, but I'm looking for Elizabeth Wakefield."

Elizabeth stood. "I'm Elizabeth Wakefield."

The man reached inside his pocket, produced a business card, and handed it to Elizabeth. "I'm Alfred Raymond, the attorney for William White's family. I've been trying to locate you for several days."

Elizabeth fell back against the bed, and Tom sat up protectively. "What do you want?" he demanded.

Mr. Raymond held up his hand. "Please, please. Don't agitate yourself. I'm aware that Mr. William White, Jr., has caused Ms. Wakefield no small degree of anxiety in the past. But in his . . . er . . . own eccentric way, he was very, very fond of Ms. Wakefield."

"So fond of her that he tried to kill her," Tom said grimly.

Mr. Raymond blinked, as if dismissing the remark as irrelevant. "I am not here as Mr. White's advocate and therefore have no comment on those events. I'm here as the executor of Mr. White's estate. As you know, Mr. White was a young man of considerable wealth. His will names only one beneficiary."

Tom lifted his eyebrow. "So?"

Mr. Raymond turned toward Elizabeth,

bowed slightly, and gave her a bland smile. "That beneficiary, Ms. Wakefield, is you."

Now that the twins have put the nightmare of William White behind them, they're ready to let loose and have some fun. Join Jessica and Elizabeth for the biggest Spring Break party ever—in Sweet Valley University #12, **COLLEGE CRUISE.**